COMIC CLASSICS

SHERLOCK HOLMES AND THE HOUND OF THE BASKERVILLES

AN OLD BOOK BY

ARTHUR CONAN DOYLE

WITH NEW DOODLES BY

JACK NOEL

Farshore

DR WATSON

(ME!)

SHERLOCK HOLMES

OUR HOME

221B

BAKER STREET

'BRILLIANT'
JENNY PEARSON

'A FUNNY, THOUGHT-PROVOKING TREAT'
GUARDIAN

'BRINGS DICKENS TO LIFE MAGNIFICENTLY'
TEENLIBRARIAN

'THOROUGHLY ENJOYABLE'
A REAL-LIFE ELEVEN-YEAR-OLD

'BRILLIANTLY WITTY'
ABI ELPHINSTONE

'GORGEOUS'
CLARE REES

'REALLY, REALLY GOOD'
SOMEONE ON AMAZON

'HILARIOUS'
THE BOOKSELLER

'HILARIOUS! JACK NOEL IS A STAR'
JIM SMITH

'WHAT A GREAT BOOK'
A REAL-LIFE NINE-YEAR-OLD

'A GEM!'
A REAL-LIFE SCHOOL LIBRARIAN

'STEVENSON'S MASTERPIECE IS BROUGHT TO LIFE'
TIMES EDUCATIONAL SUPPLEMENT

'SUCH A FANTASTIC WAY TO INTRODUCE CHILDREN TO CLASSIC AUTHORS!'
BOOKS FOR BOYS

'A REAL BOOTY OF A BOOK!'
UK MUMS TV

With thanks/apologies to Arthur Conan Doyle

ORIGINAL STORY BY **ARTHUR CONAN DOYLE** ABRIDGED BY **LUCY COURTENAY** DESIGNED AND ILLUSTRATED BY **JACK NOEL** EDITED BY **LIZ BANKES** WITH **LUCY COURTENAY** AND **ASMAA ISSE** ART-DIRECTION BY **RYAN HAMMOND** PRODUCTION **CHARLOTTE COOPER** AND TEAM FOREIGN RIGHTS **JULIETTE CLARK** AND TEAM SALES **INGRID GILMORE, DAN DOWNHAM** AND TEAM PUBLISHER **LINDSEY HEAVEN** AGENT **CLAIRE WILSON** AT RCW SPECIAL THANKS TO **CHARLOTTE KNIGHT**

First published in Great Britain in 2021 by Farshore
This edition published 2022

An imprint of HarperCollins*Publishers*
1 London Bridge Street, London SE1 9GF

farshore.co.uk

HarperCollins*Publishers*
1st Floor, Watermarque Building, Ringsend Road, Dublin 4, Ireland

Text and illustrations copyright © 2021 Jack Noel
The moral rights of the author and illustrator have been asserted

978-0-0086-0032-7
Printed and bound in the UK using 100% renewable electricity at CPI Group (UK) Ltd
1

A CIP catalogue record for this title is available from the British Library

MIX
Paper | Supporting
responsible forestry
FSC™ C007454

This book is produced from independently certified FSC™ paper
to ensure responsible forest management.

For more information visit: www.harpercollins.co.uk/green

NAME

Dr John H. Watson

AGE

29 years old

ADDRESS

221B Baker St, London

OCCUPATION:

Retired army officer.

Sherlock Holmes's Best

Friend and Assistant

ABOUT ME:

I faithfully chronicle our exploits

and detail the cases that have

been solved by Sherlock Holmes

(with my help!) so that the world

may recognise his merits.

❧ 1 ❧

The CURSE *of the* BASKERVILLES

MR SHERLOCK HOLMES (who was usually very late in the mornings, save upon those not infrequent occasions when he was up all night) was seated at the breakfast table. I stood upon the hearth-rug and picked up the stick which a visitor had left behind the night before.

We had been out when the visitor called so this was our only sign of him.

DR JOHN WATSON
"The GREAT DETECTIVE's BEST FRIEND!"

IT'S A MYSTERY!
__STICK MAN__
Who was our mystery visitor who left behind a walking stick!

It was a fine, thick piece of wood, with a bulbous head. Just under the head was a broad silver band nearly an inch across.

To James Mortimer, M.R.C.S., from his friends of the C.C.H., 1884

Well, Watson, what do you make of our visitor's stick?

Holmes was sitting with his back to me.

How did you know what I was doing?

I said.

I believe you have eyes in the back of your head!

"I have, at least, a well-polished, silver-plated coffee-pot in front of me,"

said he.

"But, tell me, Watson, what do you make of it?"

"I think," said I, "that the owner of the stick is a successful, elderly medical man."

Interesting, though *elementary*,

said he as he took the stick and returned to his favourite corner of the settee.

DEDUCTIONS ABOUT THE STICK MAN

He is a doctor
(friends of the CCH =
Charing Cross Hospital),

amiable, unambitious
(because he left London
for the country),

he lives in the
country,

a young fellow
under thirty,

absent-minded
(because he forgot
the stick),

and the possessor
of a favourite dog.

I laughed incredulously as Sherlock Holmes
rose and paced the room.

How do you
know he has
a dog?

said I.

Now he halted by the window. "The marks of his teeth are very plainly visible. The dog's jaw, as shown in the space between these marks, is too broad in my opinion for a terrier and not broad enough for a mastiff.

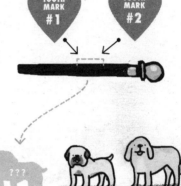

| Lil Yappy (tiny jaw) | Poodle (lil jaw) | Terrier (small jaw) | Our mystery dog | Mastiff (broad jaw) | Big boy (big jaw) |

It may have been – yes, by Jove, it is a

CURLY-HAIRED SPANIEL."

My dear fellow, how can you POSSIBLY be so sure of that?

For the very simple reason that I see the dog himself on our very door-step, and there is its owner.

COME IN!

As the man entered his eyes fell upon the stick in Holmes's hand, and he ran towards it. "I am so very glad," said he. "I would not lose that stick for the world."

The man introduced himself as Dr James Mortimer from Devonshire.

I came to you, Mr Holmes, because I am suddenly confronted with a most serious and extraordinary problem.

I have in my pocket a manuscript.

I observed it as you entered the room.

Classic Sherlock!

It is an old manuscript,

said Dr Mortimer.

Early eighteenth century, unless it is a forgery.

There he goes again!

"It was given to me by Sir Charles Baskerville," said Dr Mortimer, "whose sudden and tragic death some three months ago created so much excitement in

Devonshire Daily

LOCAL GUY KICKS THE BUCKET

Devonshire. The manuscript is a statement of a legend which runs in the Baskerville family – Sir Charles took it very seriously."

READ THE LEGEND!

Baskerville Hall 1742

One century ago, at the time of the Civil War,
Baskerville Hall was owned by Hugo Baskerville.

He was a most wild, profane, and godless man.

It chanced that this Hugo came to love the daughter of a farmer who held lands near the Baskerville estate.

But the young maiden would always avoid him, for she feared his evil name.

So it came to pass that one September night this Hugo, with five or six of his wicked companions, stole down upon the farm and carried off the maiden.

When they had brought her to the Hall the maiden was placed in an upper chamber, while Hugo and his friends sat down to drink.

Now, the poor lass upstairs was braver than they thought,

for by the aid of the ivy which covered (and still covers) the south wall she came down from a window,

and so escaped homeward across the moor.

Some little time later Hugo went to see his captive, and so found the cage empty and the bird escaped.

Then he became as one that hath a devil.

Rushing down the stairs into the dining-hall, he sprang upon the great table, and he cried out:

PUT the HOUNDS UPON HER!

Giving the hounds a handkerchief
of the maid's, so they would have
her scent, he galloped
out in the moonlight
over the moor.

Sniff!

Hugo's friends took their horses and started in pursuit.

So the squires rode onward.

But soon their skins turned cold, for there came a galloping
across the moor, and Hugo's horse, dabbled with white froth,
went past with a trailing bridle and an empty saddle.

*Then the riders rode close together,
for a great fear was on them.*

*Riding slowly
they came
at last upon
the hounds.*

*The dogs, though known for their bravery,
were whimpering in a cluster with staring eyes,
gazing down the narrow valley before them.*

*The moon was shining
bright upon the clearing, and
there in the centre lay . . .*

the body of HUGO BASKERVILLE.

But it was not this which raised the hair upon their heads, it was what stood over Hugo, plucking at his throat.

A foul thing, a great, black beast, shaped like a HOUND, yet larger than any hound that ever mortal eye has rested upon.

And even as they looked, the thing TORE THE THROAT out of Hugo Baskerville,

and it turned its *BLAZING EYES* and *DRIPPING JAWS* upon them.

The friends shrieked with fear and rode for dear life, still screaming, across the moor.

One, it is said, died that very night of what he had seen, and the other two were broken men for the rest of their days.

Such is the tale of the coming of the Hound which is said to have plagued the family ever since. So many of the Baskervilles have suffered SUDDEN, BLOODY, and MYSTERIOUS deaths.
I hereby command you to forbear from crossing the moor in those dark hours when the powers of EVIL are EXALTED.

Dr Mortimer drew a folded newspaper out of his pocket. "Now, Mr Holmes, we will give you something a little more recent. This is a short account of the death of Sir Charles Baskerville . . ."

The sudden death of Sir Charles Baskerville has cast a gloom over the county. Sir Charles, as is well known, is very rich. It is only two years since he took up his residence at Baskerville Hall. *Foul play?* There is no reason whatever to suspect foul play. Sir Charles's health has for some time been impaired.

Sir Charles (when he was still alive)

Continued on page 94

"The facts of the case are simple," Dr Mortimer read. "Sir Charles Baskerville was in the habit every night before bed of walking down the famous

Yew Alley of Baskerville Hall. On the night of the 4th of May he went out as usual. He never returned. Halfway down this walk there is a gate which leads out on to the moor. Sir Charles had stood for some little time here. He then proceeded down the Alley, and it was at the far end of it that his body was discovered. The footprints altered from the time that he passed the moor-gate, and he appeared from thence onward to have been walking upon his toes.

No signs of violence were to be discovered upon Sir Charles's person.

It is understood that the next of kin is Mr Henry Baskerville, the son of Sir Charles Baskerville's younger brother."

NEXT OF KIN

Sir Charles' closest relative is Henry Baaskerville. This means that he inherits Sir Charles's house.

Dr Mortimer refolded his paper and replaced it in his pocket.

Those are the public facts, Mr Holmes.

Then let me have the private ones,

said Sherlock Holmes.

Dr Mortimer had begun to show signs of some strong emotion. "With you there is no reason why I should not be perfectly frank.

"The moor is very sparsely inhabited, and those who live near each other are thrown very much together. For this reason I saw a good deal of Sir Charles Baskerville. With the exception of Mr Frankland, of Lafter Hall, and Mr Stapleton, the naturalist,

MR FRANKLAND
OF LAFTER HALL

and his sister, there are no others within many miles.

MR STAPLETON
THE NATURALIST

"Within the last few months, Sir Charles was strained to the breaking point. He had taken this legend which I have read you exceedingly to heart – nothing would induce him to go out upon the moor at night. He was honestly convinced that a dreadful fate overhung his family. On more than one occasion he has asked me whether I had ever seen any strange creature or heard the baying of a hound.

MR BARRYMORE
SIR CHARLES'S BUTLER

"On the night of Sir Charles's death, Barrymore the butler sent to me.

— Naturalist as in he likes nature (not getting naked)

Doc, it's Sir Charles . . .

I'll come right away

I was able to reach Baskerville Hall within an hour of the event. I carefully examined the body, which had not been touched until my arrival. Sir Charles lay on his face, his arms out, his fingers dug into the ground, and his features convulsed to such an extent that I could hardly have sworn to his identity. There was no physical injury of any kind. But one false statement was made by Barrymore at the inquest. He said that there were no traces upon the ground round the body. He did not observe any. But I did."

"Footprints?"

"Footprints."

"A man's or a woman's?"

Dr Mortimer's voice sank almost to a whisper:

Mr Holmes, they were the footprints of a gigantic hound!

A T THESE WORDS a shudder passed through me. Holmes leaned forward and his eyes had the hard, dry glitter which shot from them when he was keenly interested.

"You saw this?"

As clearly as I see you. The marks were some twenty yards from the body and no one gave them a thought.

I don't suppose I should have done so had I not known this legend.

 **What sort of night was it?**

"Damp and raw."

"What is the Alley like? I understand that the yew hedge has a gate?"

"Yes, the wicket-gate which leads on to the moor."

"The marks which you saw – were they on the same side of the path as the moor-gate?"

"Yes."

"You interest me exceedingly. Was the wicket-gate closed?"

"Closed and padlocked."

"How high was it?"

"About four feet high."

"Then anyone could have got over it?"

"Yes."

"And what marks did you see by the wicket-gate?"

"It was all very confused. Sir Charles had evidently stood there for five or ten minutes because the ash had twice dropped from his cigar."

Sherlock Holmes struck his hand against his knee with an impatient gesture.

If I had only been there!

he cried.

Slap!

It is evidently a case of extraordinary interest.

Oh, to think that you should not have called me in!

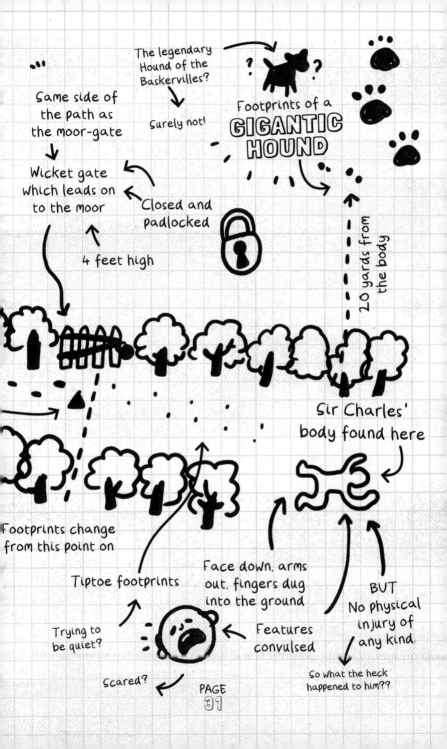

The legendary Hound of the Baskervilles?

Surely not!

Footprints of a **GIGANTIC HOUND**

Same side of the path as the moor-gate

Wicket gate which leads on to the moor

Closed and padlocked

4 feet high

20 yards from the body

Sir Charles' body found here

Footprints change from this point on

Tiptoe footprints

Trying to be quiet?

Face down, arms out, fingers dug into the ground

Features convulsed

BUT No physical injury of any kind.

So what the heck happened to him??

Scared?

"I could not call you in, Mr Holmes, without disclosing these facts to the world. Besides – there is a realm in which the most experienced of detectives is helpless."

You mean that the thing is supernatural?

"Before the terrible event occurred several people had seen a creature upon the moor which corresponds with this Baskerville demon. They all agreed that it was a huge creature, luminous, ghastly, and spectral ..."

"And you, a trained man of science, believe it to be supernatural?"

"I do not know what to believe."

Holmes shrugged his shoulders.

Then, how can I assist you?

"By advising me as to what I should do with SIR HENRY BASKERVILLE, who arrives at Waterloo Station" – Dr Mortimer looked at his watch – "in exactly one hour and a quarter."

"He being the heir?"

"Yes. We found that he had been farming in Canada. From the accounts which have reached us he is an excellent fellow in every way."

SIR HENRY BASKERVILLE
AN EXCELLENT FELLOW
IN EVERY WAY

"There are no other Baskervilles?"

"None. The only other whom we have been able to trace was Rodger Baskerville, the youngest of three brothers of whom poor Sir Charles was the elder. The second brother, who died young, is the father of Sir Henry. The third, Rodger, was the black sheep of the family. He was the very image, they tell me, of the family picture of old Hugo. He fled to Central America, and died there in 1876 of yellow fever."

THE BASKERVILLE BROTHERS

CHARLES BASKERVILLE
Recently died at Baskerville Hall

MIDDLE BROTHER
He died young.

RODGER BASKERVILLE
Looked just like Hugo.
Died in 1876.

HENRY BASKERVILLE
Son of the middle brother. Nice guy.

(BTW this book is set in 1889!)

"Sir Henry is the last of the Baskervilles. In one hour and five minutes I meet him at Waterloo Station. Now, Mr Holmes, what would you advise me to do with him?" said Dr Mortimer.

Why should he not go to Baskerville Hall, the home of his fathers?

said Holmes.

Every Baskerville who goes there meets with an EVIL FATE. I feel sure that if Sir Charles could have spoken with me before his death he would have warned me against bringing the heir to that deadly place.

And yet it cannot be denied that the prosperity of the whole poor, bleak countryside depends upon his presence.

WHAT SHOULD I DO WITH HENRY?

Take him to Baskerville Hall where he might be in danger?

Keep him away from the hall, meaning the whole area will lose money and jobs as the locals depend on someone running the estate?

Holmes considered for a little time.

"I recommend, sir, that you proceed to Waterloo to meet Sir Henry Baskerville. You will say nothing to him at all until I have made up my mind about the matter.

"At ten o'clock tomorrow, Dr Mortimer, you will call upon me here, and you will bring Sir Henry Baskerville with you."

"I will do so, Mr Holmes." He scribbled the appointment on his shirtcuff and hurried off.

~~Buy milk~~
~~Find stick~~
Bring Henry to see
Holmes at Baker
Street, 10am

Holmes stopped him at the head of the stair.

"Only one more question, Dr Mortimer. You say that before Sir Charles Baskerville's death several people saw this apparition upon the moor?"

"Three people did."

I saw it! Scared me half to death.

A massive mutt, it was!

A terrifying ghost hound!

"Did any of them see it after his death?"

"I have not heard of any."

"Thank you. Good morning."

I spent the day at my club and did not return to Baker Street until evening.

Yes, I have my own life without Sherlock, thank you very much

BACK AT BAKER STREET

My first impression as I opened the door was that a fire had broken out, for the room was filled with smoke. Through the haze I had a vague vision of Holmes in his dressing-gown coiled up in an armchair with his black clay pipe between his lips.

I HAVE BEEN TO DEVONSHIRE! he said.

In spirit?

Exactly. After you left I sent for the map of this portion of the moor, and my spirit has hovered over it all day.

He unrolled one section and held it over his knee.

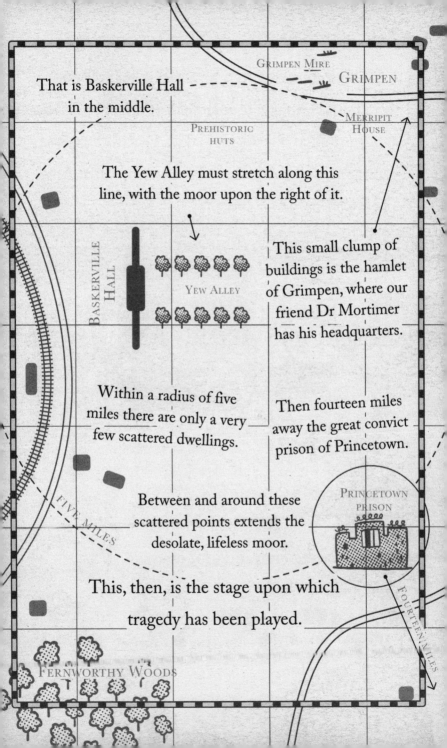

That is Baskerville Hall in the middle.

GRIMPEN MIRE

GRIMPEN

PREHISTORIC HUTS

MERRIPIT HOUSE

The Yew Alley must stretch along this line, with the moor upon the right of it.

BASKERVILLE HALL

YEW ALLEY

This small clump of buildings is the hamlet of Grimpen, where our friend Dr Mortimer has his headquarters.

Within a radius of five miles there are only a very few scattered dwellings.

Then fourteen miles away the great convict prison of Princetown.

Between and around these scattered points extends the desolate, lifeless moor.

PRINCETOWN PRISON

This, then, is the stage upon which tragedy has been played.

FIVE MILES

FOURTEEN MILES

FERNWORTHY WOODS

"There are two questions waiting for us," said Holmes. "The one is whether any crime has been committed at all; the second is, what is the crime and how was it committed? Have you turned the case over in your mind?"

"It is very bewildering," I said.

"It has certainly a character of its own. That change in the footprints, for example. What do you make of that?"

Normal footprints

Different footprints – but why?

"Mortimer said that Sir Charles had walked on tiptoe."

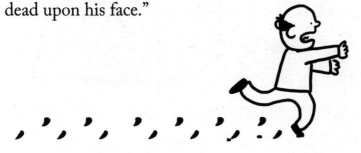

"Why should a man walk on tiptoe? He was running, Watson – RUNNING FOR HIS LIFE, running until he burst his heart and fell dead upon his face."

"Running from what?"

"There lies our problem. There are indications that the man was crazed with fear. I am presuming that the cause of his fears came to him across the moor. Whom was he waiting for that night?"

"You think that he was waiting for someone?"

"The man was elderly and infirm. The ground was damp and the night inclement. Is it natural that he should stand for five or ten minutes?"

"But he went out every evening."

"I think it unlikely that he waited at the moor-gate every evening. He avoided the moor. That night he waited there. The thing

IT'S A MYSTERY!
SIR CHARLES
Was Charles waiting
at the moor-gate to
meet someone?
Who??

takes shape, Watson. Might I ask you to hand me my violin, and we will postpone all further thought upon this business until we have had the advantage of meeting Dr Mortimer and Sir Henry Baskerville in the morning."

(He says playing
the violin helps
him think)

SIR HENRY BASKERVILLE

THE CLOCK HAD just struck ten when
Dr Mortimer was shown up, followed
by a small, alert, dark-eyed man about thirty
years of age, very sturdily built,
with thick black eyebrows and
a strong, pugnacious face. He
wore a ruddy-tinted tweed suit
and had the weather-beaten
appearance of one who has
spent most of his time in the open air.

> **PUGNACIOUS**
> Someone who loves drama and always starting arguments
>
> **PUGS**
> Super cute doggos

This is
SIR HENRY
BASKERVILLE,

said Dr
Mortimer.

"I understand that you think out little puzzles, Mr Holmes," said Sir Henry, "and I've had one this morning."

It was this letter, which reached me this morning.

"Who knew that you were going to the Northumberland Hotel?" asked Holmes.

"No one could have known."

"Hum! Someone seems to be very deeply interested in your movements." Out of the envelope he took a half-sheet of foolscap paper folded into four. This he opened and spread flat upon the table. A single sentence had been formed by pasting printed words upon it.

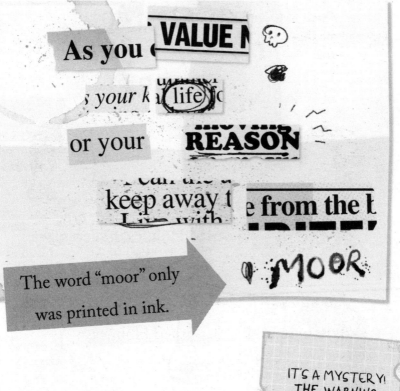

As you VALUE

s your k life

or your REASON

keep away from the

MOOR

The word "moor" only was printed in ink.

IT'S A MYSTERY!
THE WARNING
Who sent Sir Henry the strange note?

"Have you yesterday's *Times*, Watson? The inside page, please, with the leading articles?" said Sherlock Holmes.

He glanced swiftly over it.

What do you think of that, Watson?

cried Holmes in high glee.

I confess that I see no connection.

 "And yet, my dear Watson, there is so very close a connection that the one is extracted out of the other.

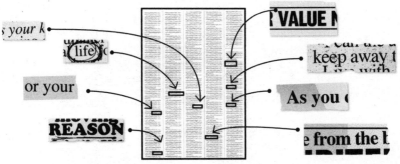

Don't you see now whence these words have been taken?"

By thunder, you're right! Well, if that isn't smart!

cried Sir Henry.

 "If any possible doubt remained it is settled by the fact that 'keep away' and 'from the' are cut out in one piece."

"Well, now – so it is!"

"But I want to know why the word 'moor' should have been written?" said Dr Mortimer

"Because he could not find it in print."

"Why, of course, that would explain it. Have you read anything else in this message, Mr Holmes?"

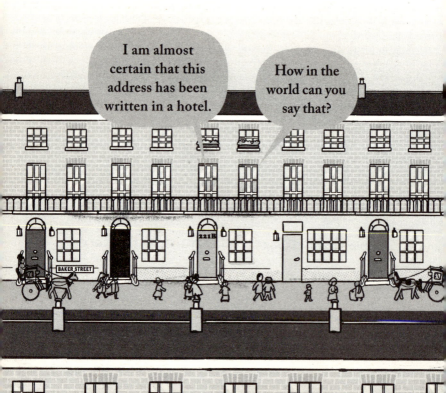

"Both the pen and the ink have given the writer trouble.

The pen has spluttered twice in a single word,

and has run dry three times in a short address, showing that there was very little ink in the bottle.

Now, a private pen or ink-bottle is seldom allowed to be in such a state, and the combination of the two must be quite rare. But you know the hotel ink and the hotel pen, where it is rare to get anything else," said Holmes.

"Sir Henry, has anything else of interest happened to you since you have been in London?"

"Well, it depends upon what you think worth reporting."

"I think anything out of the ordinary routine of life well worth reporting."

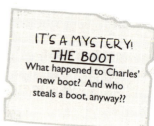

LOST

Brown boot (just one)
** Never worn! **

Sir Henry smiled. "I hope that to lose one of your boots is not part of the ordinary routine of life over here."

"You have lost one of your boots?"

"Well, mislaid it, anyhow. I put them both outside my door last night, and there was only one in the morning. The worst of it is that I only bought the pair last night on the Strand, and I have never had them on."

IT'S A MYSTERY!
THE BOOT
What happened to Charles'
new boot? And who
steals a boot, anyway??

"It seems a singularly useless thing to steal," said Sherlock Holmes.

Not entirely useless!

"And, now, gentlemen," said the baronet with decision, "it is time that you kept your promise and gave me a full account of what we are all driving at."

"Your request is a very reasonable one," Holmes answered. "Dr Mortimer, tell your story as you told it to us."

Our scientific friend drew his papers from his pocket, and presented the whole case as he had done upon the morning before.

Sir Henry Baskerville listened with the deepest attention, and with an occasional exclamation of surprise.

"Well, I seem to have come into an inheritance with a vengeance," said he when the long narrative was finished. "Of course, I've heard of the Hound ever since I was in the nursery.

It's the pet story of the family, though I never thought of taking it seriously before. And now there's this letter to me at the hotel. I suppose that fits into place."

"It seems to show that someone knows more than we do about what goes on upon the moor," said Dr Mortimer.

"And also," said Holmes, "that someone is not ill-disposed towards you, since they warn you of danger. But the practical point which we now have to decide, Sir Henry, is whether it is or is not advisable for you to go to Baskerville Hall."

"Why should I not go?"

"There seems to be danger."

There is no DEVIL in HELL, Mr Holmes, and there is no man upon earth who can prevent me from going to the home of my own people.

His dark brows knitted and his face flushed to a dusky red as he spoke.

It was evident that the fiery temper of the Baskervilles was not extinct.

"It's half-past eleven now and I am going back right away to my hotel. Suppose you come round and lunch with us at two. I'll be able to tell you more clearly then how this thing strikes me," said Sir Henry.

"Is that convenient to you, Watson?"

"Perfectly."

Then we meet again at two o'clock. Au revoir, and good-morning!

We heard the steps of our visitors descend the stair and the bang of the front door.

SLAM!

In an instant Holmes had changed from the languid dreamer to the man of action.

Your hat and boots, Watson, quick!

Not a moment to lose!

We hurried together down the stairs and into the street. Dr Mortimer and Baskerville were still visible about two hundred yards ahead of us in the direction of Oxford Street.

Holmes quickened his pace until we had decreased the distance which divided us by about half.

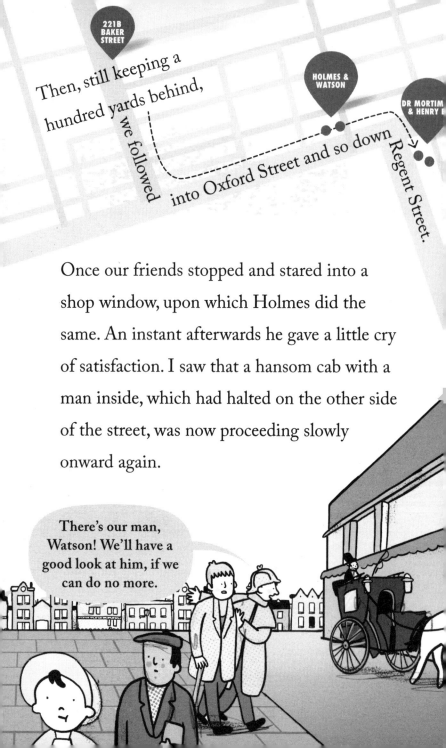

221B BAKER STREET

HOLMES & WATSON

DR MORTIM & HENRY

Then, still keeping a hundred yards behind, we followed into Oxford Street and so down Regent Street.

Once our friends stopped and stared into a shop window, upon which Holmes did the same. An instant afterwards he gave a little cry of satisfaction. I saw that a hansom cab with a man inside, which had halted on the other side of the street, was now proceeding slowly onward again.

There's our man, Watson! We'll have a good look at him, if we can do no more.

A bushy black beard and a pair of piercing eyes turned upon us through the side window of the cab.

The cab flew madly off down Regent Street. Holmes dashed in wild pursuit amid the stream of the traffic, but the start was too great, and already the cab was out of sight.

"There now!" said Holmes bitterly. "Was there ever such bad luck?"

"Who was the man?" said I.

"I have not an idea."

"A spy?"

> IT'S A MYSTERY!
> ## THE MAN IN THE CAB
> Who's the beardy guy in the cab who's following Henry?

"Sir Henry has been very closely shadowed by someone since he has been in town. We are dealing with a clever man, Watson."

What a pity we did not get the number of the cab!

"My dear Watson, you surely do not seriously imagine that I neglected to get the number? No. 2704 is our man. Could you swear to that man's face within the cab?"

IT'S A MYSTERY!
THE MAN IN THE CAB
The cab's licence plate was 2704

"I could swear only to the beard."

"And so could I – from which I gather that in all probability it was a false one. Come in here, Watson!"

He turned into one of the district messenger offices, where he was warmly greeted by the manager.

Why it's Sherlock Holmes!

DISTRICT MESSENGERS

Kids and teens who were employed to run urgent tasks or carry messages through urban streets. These days we use WhatsApp.

"I have some recollection, Wilson, that you had among your boys a lad named Cartwright, who showed some ability during an investigation."

Yes, sir, he is still with us.

← Wilson – the manager

"Could you ring him up?"

A lad of fourteen, with a bright, keen face, had obeyed the summons of the manager. He stood now gazing with great reverence at the famous detective.

"Let me have the Hotel Directory," said Holmes. "Thank you! Now, Cartwright, there are the names of

twenty-three hotels here, all in the immediate neighbourhood of Charing Cross. Do you see?"

"Yes, sir."

You will visit each of these in turn. You will tell them that you want to see the waste-paper of yesterday.

You will say that an important telegram has gone astray and that you are looking for it.

You understand?

Yes, sir.

"But what you are really looking for is the centre page of the Times

Let me have a report by wire at Baker Street

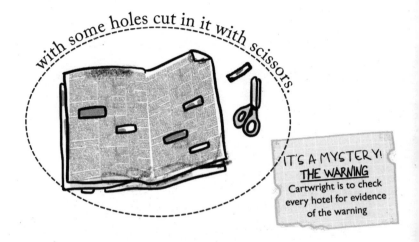

with some holes cut in it with scissors

IT'S A MYSTERY!
THE WARNING
Cartwright is to check every hotel for evidence of the warning

before evening. And now, Watson, it only remains for us to find out the identity of the cabman, No. 2704, and then we will drop into one of the Bond Street picture galleries and fill in the time until we are due at the hotel."

HANSOM CAB CO
#2704

S HERLOCK HOLMES HAD the power of
detaching his mind at will. For two hours
he was entirely absorbed in the pictures. He
would talk of nothing but art from our leaving
the gallery until we found ourselves at the
Northumberland Hotel.

What was your
favourite painting
Watson?

Er . . . shouldn't
we think about
the mystery??

As we came round the top of the stairs we had run up against Sir Henry Baskerville himself. His face was flushed with anger, and he held an old and dusty boot in one of his hands.

Seems to me they are playing me for a **SUCKER** in this hotel,

he cried.

They'll find they've started to monkey with the wrong man unless they are careful.

By thunder, if that chap can't find my missing boot there will be trouble.

But, surely, you said that it was a new brown boot?

So it was, sir.

And now it's an old black one.

LOST

Brown boot (one)
Never worn

What! you don't mean to say . . . ?

IT'S A MYSTERY!
THE BOOT
Now someone has taken his old black boot. But who . . . and why?

"That's just what I do mean to say.

Last night they took one of my brown ones,

and today they have sneaked one of the black.

It's the last thing of mine that I'll lose in this den of thieves. Well, well, Mr Holmes, you'll excuse my troubling you about such a trifle . . ."

"I think it's well worth troubling about," said Holmes, thoughtfully. "This case of yours is very complex, Sir Henry. We hold several threads in our hands, and the odds are that one or other of them guides us to the truth. We may waste time in following the wrong one, but sooner or later we must come upon the right."

We had a pleasant luncheon in which little was said of the business which had brought us together. Then Holmes asked Baskerville what his intentions were.

So what's your plan, Henry?

To go to **BASKERVILLE HALL** at the end of the week.

"On the whole," said Holmes, "I think that your decision is a wise one. I have ample evidence that you are being dogged in London. You did not know, Dr Mortimer, that you were followed this morning from my house?"

Dr Mortimer started violently.

Followed! By whom?

"That, unfortunately, is what I cannot tell you. Have you among your neighbours or acquaintances on Dartmoor any man with a black, full beard?"

"Barrymore, Sir Charles's butler, is a man with a full, black beard." ⟶

MR BARRYMORE
SIR CHARLES'S BUTLER
BIG BLACK BEARD

"Ha! Where is Barrymore?"

"He is in charge of the Hall."

"We had best ascertain if he is really there. Give me a telegraph form. Address to

Mr Barrymore, Baskerville Hall. We will send a second wire to the postmaster: 'Telegram to Mr Barrymore to be delivered into his own hand.

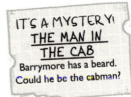

IT'S A MYSTERY!
__THE MAN IN__
__THE CAB__
Barrymore has a beard.
Could he be the cabman?

Remember this guy . . . who is he?

If absent, please return wire to Sir Henry Baskerville, Northumberland Hotel.' That should let us know before evening whether Barrymore is at his post in Devonshire or not."

"That's so," said Baskerville. "By the way, Dr Mortimer, who is this Barrymore?"

MRS BARRYMORE
BARRYMORE'S WIFE
(ALSO A PERSON IN HER OWN RIGHT)

> IT'S A MYSTERY!
> ## THE MAN IN THE CAB
> By sending a telegram that has to be received in person we'll find out if Barrymore is at the Hall!

"He is the son of the old caretaker, who is dead. His family have looked after the Hall for four generations now. So far as I know, he and his wife are as respectable a couple as any in the county."

Did Barrymore profit at all by Sir Charles's will?

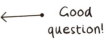
Good question!

asked Holmes.

"He and his wife had five hundred pounds each."

£500 for BARRYMORE

£500 for MRS BARRYMORE

"That is very interesting."

"I also had a thousand pounds left to me," said Dr Mortimer.

"Indeed! And anyone else?"

£1000 for DR MORTIMER

for THE POSTMAN

"There were many insignificant sums to individuals, and a large number of public charities.

for THE DONKEY SANCTUARY

for THE DEVON DOGS' HOME

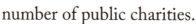
The residue all went to Sir Henry."

"And how much was the residue?"

"SEVEN HUNDRED AND FORTY THOUSAND POUNDS."

£740,000 FOR SIR HENRY BASKERVILLE (!)

Holmes raised his eyebrows in surprise.

Dear me!
It is a stake for which
a man might well play a
desperate game.

"Well, Sir Henry," said Holmes, "I am of one mind with you as to your going down to Devonshire without delay. There is only one provision which I must make. You must take with you someone, a trusty man, who will be always by your side."

Is it possible
that you could
come yourself,
Mr Holmes?

"With my extensive consulting practice it is impossible for me to be absent from London for an indefinite time."

"Whom would you recommend, then?"

Holmes laid his hand upon my arm.

"If my friend would undertake it there is no man who is better worth having at your side when you are in a tight place."

Baskerville seized me by the hand and wrung it heartily.

Well, now, that is REAL KIND of you, Dr Watson,

said he.

If you will come down to Baskerville Hall and see me through I'll never forget it.

The promise of adventure had always a fascination for me.

"I will come, with pleasure."

"Then on Saturday, we shall meet at the 10:30 train from Paddington."

We had risen to depart when Baskerville gave a cry, of triumph, and diving into one of the corners of the room he drew a brown boot from under a cabinet.

MY MISSING BOOT! he cried.

↑ Well, one of them (the new brown one)

"May all our difficulties vanish as easily!" said Sherlock Holmes.

"But it is a very singular thing," Dr Mortimer remarked. "I searched this room carefully before lunch."

"And so did I," said Baskerville. "Every inch of it. There was certainly no boot in it then."

Another item had been added to that series of small mysteries which had succeeded each other so rapidly. Setting aside Sir Charles's death, we had a line of inexplicable incidents all within the limits of two days:

- the receipt of the printed letter
- the black-bearded spy in the hansom
- the loss of the new brown boot
- the loss of the old black boot
- and now the return of the new brown boot.

Holmes sat in silence in the cab as we drove back to Baker Street. All afternoon and late into the evening he sat lost in tobacco and thought. Just before dinner two telegrams were handed in. The first ran:

The second:

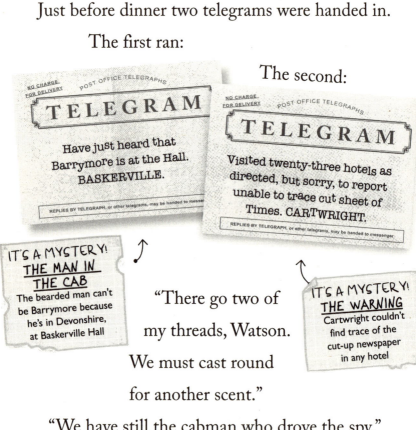

TELEGRAM

Have just heard that Barrymore is at the Hall. BASKERVILLE.

TELEGRAM

Visited twenty-three hotels as directed, but sorry, to report unable to trace cut sheet of Times. CARTWRIGHT.

IT'S A MYSTERY!
THE MAN IN THE CAB
The bearded man can't be Barrymore because he's in Devonshire, at Baskerville Hall

IT'S A MYSTERY!
THE WARNING
Cartwright couldn't find trace of the cut-up newspaper in any hotel

"There go two of my threads, Watson. We must cast round for another scent."

"We have still the cabman who drove the spy."

"Exactly. I have wired to get his name and address from the Official Registry.

Hello, who's this?

DING DONG!

"I should not be surprised if this were an answer to my question."

The ring at the bell proved to be something even more satisfactory than an answer, however, for the door opened and a rough-looking fellow entered who was evidently the cabman himself.

I got a message from the head office that a gent at this address had been inquiring for 2704, said he.

I've driven my cab this seven years and never a word of complaint.

I came here straight from the Yard to ask you to your face what you had against me.

"I have nothing in the world against you, my good man," said Holmes. "On the contrary, I have half a sovereign for you if you will give me a clear answer to my questions."

← Half a sovereign

Well, I've had a good day and no mistake,

said the cabman, with a grin.

What was it you wanted to ask, sir?

"First of all your name and address, in case I want you again."

"John Clayton, 3 Turpey Street, the Borough." Sherlock Holmes made a note of it.

"Now, Clayton, tell me all about the passenger who came and watched this house at ten o'clock this morning and afterwards followed the two gentlemen down Regent Street."

The man looked surprised. "The gentleman told me that he was a detective," said he.

"Did he say anything more?"

"He mentioned his name."

Holmes cast a swift glance of triumph at me. "Oh, he mentioned his name, did he? That was imprudent. What was the name that he mentioned?"

His name, said the cabman, was **MR SHERLOCK HOLMES.**

My name? Sherlock Holmes!!

Never have I seen my friend more completely taken aback than by the cabman's reply. Then he burst into a hearty laugh. —→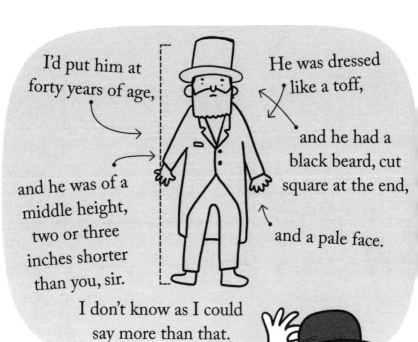

"So his name was Sherlock Holmes, was it?"

"Yes, sir, that was the gentleman's name."

"And how would you describe Mr Sherlock Holmes?"

The cabman scratched his head.

I'd put him at forty years of age, and he was of a middle height, two or three inches shorter than you, sir.

He was dressed like a toff, and he had a black beard, cut square at the end, and a pale face.

I don't know as I could say more than that.

"Well, then, here is your half-sovereign. There's another one waiting for you if you can bring any more information. Good night!"

"Good night, sir, and thank you!"

John Clayton departed chuckling, and Holmes turned to me with a shrug of his shoulders and a rueful smile.

"Snap goes our third thread, and we end where we began," said he. "The cunning rascal! I tell you, Watson, this time we have got a foeman who is worthy of our steel. I've been checkmated in London."

IT'S A MYSTERY!
THE MAN IN
THE CAB
The cab driver didn't
help much!

"I can only wish you better luck in Devonshire. But I'm not easy in my mind about it."

"About what?"

"About sending you. It's an ugly business, Watson, an ugly dangerous business, and the more I see of it the less I like it. Yes, my dear fellow, you may laugh, but I give you my word that I shall be very glad to have you back safe and sound in Baker Street once more."

5

BASKERVILLE HALL

S IR HENRY BASKERVILLE and Dr Mortimer were ready, and we started for Devonshire. Mr Sherlock Holmes drove with me to the station and gave me his last parting advice.

I will not bias your mind by suggesting theories or suspicions, Watson,

said he;

I wish you simply to report facts in the fullest possible manner to me, and you can leave me to do the theorising.

What sort of facts?

I asked.

"Anything which may seem to have a bearing, however indirect, upon the case – and especially the relations between young Sir Henry Baskerville and his neighbours or any fresh particulars concerning the death of Sir Charles."

"Would it not be well in the first place to get rid of this Barrymore?" said I.

"No, no, we will preserve him upon our list of suspects.

THE UNUSUAL SUSPECTS

There is our friend Dr Mortimer, and there is his wife.

There is Mr Frankland, of Lafter Hall,

Our friends had already secured a first-class carriage and were waiting for us upon the platform.

"I beg, Sir Henry," said Holmes, "that you will not go about alone. Some great misfortune will befall you if you do. Did you get your other boot?"

IT'S A MYSTERY!
THE BOOT
The new boot came back, but the old one is still missing …

"No, sir, it is gone forever."

"Indeed. That is very interesting. Well, good-bye," he added as the train began to glide down the platform.

Bear in mind, Sir Henry, one of the phrases in that old legend Dr Mortimer read to us, and AVOID THE MOOR in those hours of darkness when the powers of evil are exalted.

The journey was a swift and pleasant one,

and I spent it in making the more intimate acquaintance of my two companions and in playing with Dr Mortimer's spaniel. Sir Henry stared eagerly out of the window, and cried aloud with delight as he recognised the familiar features of the Devon scenery.

I'm as keen as possible to see the moor, said he.

"Then your wish is easily granted, for there is your first sight of the moor," said Dr Mortimer, pointing out of the carriage window.

There rose in the distance a grey, melancholy hill, with a strange jagged summit, dim and vague in the distance, like some fantastic landscape in a dream. Baskerville sat for a long time, his eyes fixed upon it, and I read upon his eager face how much it meant to him.

Well, if I _have_ to go out on this dangerous moor (that's possibly haunted by a spooky dog) . . .

. . . this guy seems like a good one to go with.

The train pulled up at a small wayside station and we all descended. Outside, a wagonette with a pair of cobs was waiting.

A cob is a type of horse (I had to look that up)

The coachman, a hard-faced, gnarled little fellow, saluted Sir Henry Baskerville, and in a few minutes we were flying swiftly down the broad, white road.

Rolling pasture lands curved upward on either side of us, and old gabled houses peeped out from amid the thick green foliage,

but behind the peaceful and sunlit countryside there rose the long, gloomy curve of the moor, broken by the jagged and sinister hills.

"Halloa!" cried Dr Mortimer, "what is this?"

A steep curve of heath-clad land lay in front of us. On the summit was a mounted soldier, dark and stern, his rifle poised ready over his forearm. He was watching the road along which we travelled.

What is this, Perkins?

asked Dr Mortimer.

Our driver half turned in his seat. "There's a convict escaped from Princetown, sir.

The Devonshire Daily

NOTTING HILL MURDERER ESCAPES FROM PRISON

"A man that would stick at nothing."

"[He] looks nothing like Hugh Grant"

He's been out three days now, and the warders watch every road, but they've had no sight of him yet. The farmers about here don't like it, sir, and that's a fact. You see, it isn't like any ordinary convict. This is a man that would stick at nothing."

Who is he, then?

It is **SELDEN,** the Notting Hill murderer.

In front of us rose the huge expanse
of the moor, mottled with gnarled
and craggy cairns and tors.

A cold wind

swept down from it

and set us shivering.

Somewhere there, on that desolate plain, was lurking this fiendish man, hiding in a burrow like a wild beast.

The Notting Hill murderer could be hiding anywhere!

Here??

Or here . . .

Or even here . . .

Even Baskerville fell silent and pulled his overcoat more closely around him.

The road in front of us grew bleaker and wilder. Now and then we passed a moorland cottage, walled and roofed with stone, with no creeper to break its harsh outline.

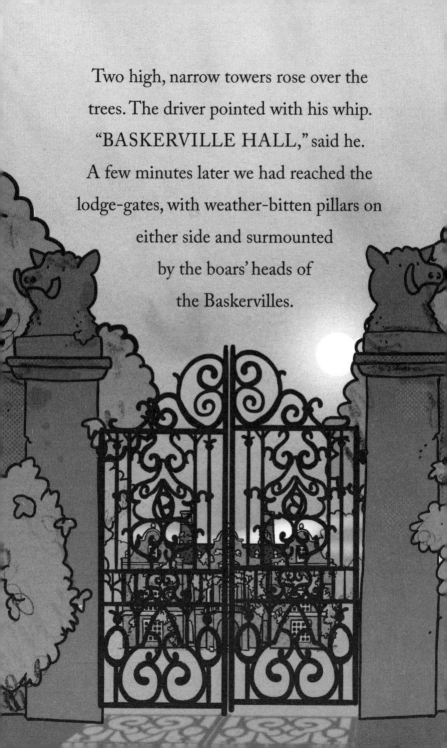

Two high, narrow towers rose over the
trees. The driver pointed with his whip.
"BASKERVILLE HALL," said he.
A few minutes later we had reached the
lodge-gates, with weather-bitten pillars on
either side and surmounted
by the boars' heads of
the Baskervilles.

Through the gateway we passed into the avenue, and the old trees shot their branches in a sombre tunnel over our heads. Baskerville shuddered as he looked up the long, dark drive to where the house glimmered like a ghost at the farther end.

he asked in a low voice.

"No, no, the Yew Alley is on the other side."

The young heir glanced round with a gloomy face.

"It's no wonder my uncle felt as if trouble were coming on him in such a place as this," said he. "It's enough to scare any man. I'll have a row of electric lamps up here inside of six months."

The avenue opened into
a broad expanse of turf,
and the house lay before us.

The whole front
was draped in ivy,
with a patch clipped
bare here and there
where a window or a
coat-of-arms broke
through the dark veil.

A dull light shone through heavy mullioned windows, and from the high chimneys there sprang a single black column of smoke.

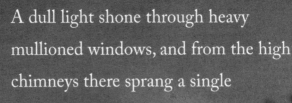

Welcome, Sir Henry!

Welcome to
BASKERVILLE HALL!

A tall man had stepped from the shadow of the porch to open the door of the wagonette. The figure of a woman was silhouetted against the yellow light of the hall. She came out and helped the man to hand down our bags.

"You don't mind my driving straight home, Sir Henry?" said Dr Mortimer. "My wife is expecting me. Good-bye, and never hesitate night or day to send for me if I can be of service."

The wheels died away down the drive while Sir Henry and I turned into the hall, and the door clanged heavily behind us.

It was large, lofty, and heavily raftered with age-blackened oak. In the great old-fashioned fireplace behind the high iron dogs a log-fire crackled and snapped.

Sir Henry and I held out our hands to it, for we were numb from our long drive.

Then we gazed round us

at the high, thin window of old stained glass,

the stags' heads,

the oak panelling,

the coats-of-arms upon the walls.

It's just as I imagined it,

said Sir Henry.

The tall man – Barrymore the butler – had returned from taking our luggage to our rooms. He was a remarkable-looking man, tall, handsome, with a square black beard.

"Would you wish dinner to be served at once, sir?"

"Is it ready?"

In a very few minutes, sir.

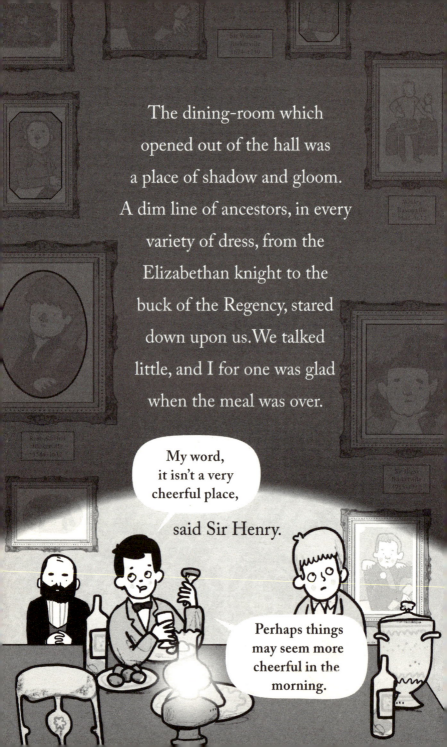

The dining-room which opened out of the hall was a place of shadow and gloom. A dim line of ancestors, in every variety of dress, from the Elizabethan knight to the buck of the Regency, stared down upon us. We talked little, and I for one was glad when the meal was over.

My word, it isn't a very cheerful place,

said Sir Henry.

Perhaps things may seem more cheerful in the morning.

AND SO TO BED

I found myself weary and yet wakeful, tossing restlessly from side to side. Far away a chiming clock struck out the quarters of the hours, but otherwise a deathly silence lay upon the old house.

And then suddenly, in the very dead of the night, there came a sound to my ears.

Boo hoo!

Sob!

Weep!

Wail!

Sniffle!

It was the sob of a woman who is torn by an uncontrollable sorrow.

I listened intently. The noise was certainly in the house. For half an hour I waited with every nerve on the alert, but there came no other sound save the chiming clock and the rustle of the ivy on the wall.

Cry!

Snivel!

Mewl!

Blub!

Lament!

More sobbing

Bawl!

Keen!

IT'S A MYSTERY!
THE WEEPING WOMAN
Who is crying in the night ... and why!?

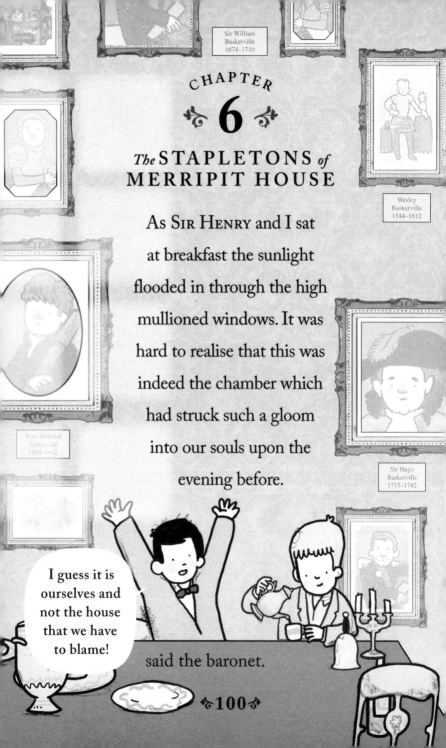

CHAPTER

6

The STAPLETONS of MERRIPIT HOUSE

As Sir Henry and I sat at breakfast the sunlight flooded in through the high mullioned windows. It was hard to realise that this was indeed the chamber which had struck such a gloom into our souls upon the evening before.

I guess it is ourselves and not the house that we have to blame!

said the baronet.

❧100❧

"And yet it was not entirely a question of imagination," I answered. "Did you happen to hear someone, a woman I think, sobbing in the night?"

I fancy that I heard something of the sort.

I waited quite a time, but there was no more of it, so I concluded that it was all a dream.

I heard it distinctly, and I am sure that it was really the sob of a woman.

"We must ask about this right away." He rang the bell and asked Barrymore whether he could account for our experience.

It seemed to me that the pallid features of the butler turned a shade paler still.

Pallid

Pasty

Ashen

Paler still

There is only one woman in the house, Sir Henry,

he answered.

That woman is my wife, and I can answer for it that the sound could not have come from her.

After breakfast I met Mrs Barrymore in the long corridor with the sun full upon her face.

Her eyes were a tell-tale red and glanced at me from between swollen lids.

Red

Pinky

Blush

Pale

It was she, then, who wept in the night, and if she did so her husband must know it. Yet he had taken the obvious risk of discovery in declaring that it was not so. Why had he done this? And why did she weep so bitterly?

IT'S A MYSTERY!
THE WEEPING WOMAN
It was Mrs Barrymore! But why did Barrymore deny it? And why was she so upset?

Was it possible that it was Barrymore after all whom we had seen in the cab in Regent Street? The beard might well have been the same . . .

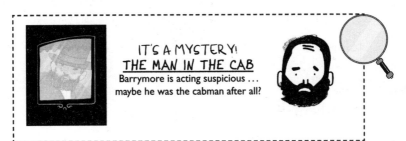

IT'S A MYSTERY!
THE MAN IN THE CAB
Barrymore is acting suspicious . . . maybe he was the cabman after all?

Obviously the first thing to do was to see the Grimpen postmaster, and find whether the test telegram had really been placed in Barrymore's own hands.

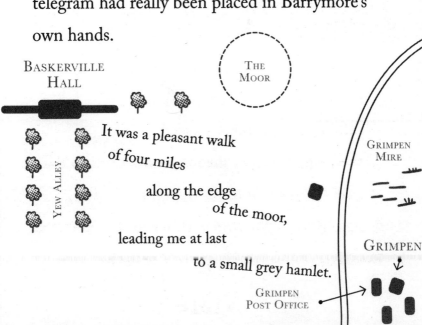

BASKERVILLE HALL

THE MOOR

It was a pleasant walk of four miles along the edge of the moor, leading me at last to a small grey hamlet.

YEW ALLEY

GRIMPEN MIRE

GRIMPEN

GRIMPEN POST OFFICE

"Certainly, sir," said the postmaster, "I had the telegram delivered to Mr Barrymore exactly as directed."

"Who delivered it?"

My boy here.

James, you delivered that telegram to Mr Barrymore at the Hall last week, did you not?

Yes, father, I delivered it.

"Into his own hands?" I asked.

"Well, he was up in the loft at the time, so that I could not put it into his own hands, but I gave it into Mrs Barrymore's hands, and she promised to deliver it at once."

Did you see Mr Barrymore?

No, sir; I tell you he was in the loft.

"If you didn't see him, how do you know he was in the loft?"

"WELL, SURELY HIS OWN WIFE OUGHT TO KNOW WHERE HE IS," said the postmaster testily. "Didn't he get the telegram? If there is any mistake it is for Mr Barrymore himself to complain."

It was clear that in spite of Holmes's ruse we had no proof that Barrymore had not been in London all the time. What interest could he have in persecuting the Baskerville family?

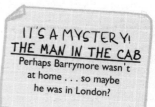

IT'S A MYSTERY!
THE MAN IN THE CAB
Perhaps Barrymore wasn't at home . . . so maybe he was in London?

Holmes himself had said that no more complex case had come to him. I prayed, as I walked back along the grey, lonely road, that my friend might soon be able to come down to take this heavy burden of responsibility from my shoulders.

Suddenly my thoughts were interrupted by the sound of running feet behind me and a voice calling my name. To my surprise it was a stranger.

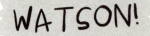

"I have been calling on Dr Mortimer, and he pointed you out to me from the window of his surgery as you passed. I thought that I would introduce myself," said Stapleton. "I trust that Sir Henry is none the worse for his journey?"

"He is very well, thank you."

"We were all rather afraid that after the sad death of Sir Charles the new baronet might refuse to live here. Sir Henry has, I suppose, no superstitious fears in the matter?"

"I do not think that it is likely."

Hello! My name is Jack Stapleton

Of course you know the legend of the fiend dog which haunts the family?

He spoke with a smile.

LOCAL LEGEND

HOUND OF THE BASKERVILLES

The story took a great hold upon the imagination of Sir Charles.

I fancy that he really did see something of the kind upon that last night in the Yew Alley.

You think, then, that some dog pursued Sir Charles, and that he died of fright?

"Have you any better explanation?"

"I have not come to any conclusion."

"Has Mr Sherlock Holmes?" ← Everyone loves Sherlock!

"I am afraid that I cannot answer that question."

"May I ask if he is going to honour us with a visit himself?"

"He cannot leave town at present. He has other cases which engage his attention."

WHAT A PITY! He might throw some light on that which is so dark to us.

But if there is any possible way in which I can be of service to you I trust that you will command me.

We had come to a point where a narrow grassy path struck off from the road and wound away across the moor.

A moderate walk along this moor-path brings us to my home, Merripit House, said he.

Perhaps you will spare an hour that I may have the pleasure of introducing you to my sister.

The Moor
Merripit House ☛
☛ Grimpen Post Office

Holmes had said that I should study the neighbours upon the moor. I accepted Stapleton's invitation, and we turned together down the path.

Be friendly and talk to everyone . . . you might learn something!

It is a wonderful place, the moor,

said he.

You cannot think the wonderful secrets which it contains. It is so vast, and so barren, and so mysterious.

You know it well, then?

"I have only been here two years. We came shortly after Sir Charles settled. But my tastes led me to explore every part of the country, and I should think that there are few men who know it better than I do."

"Is it hard to know?"

"Very hard. You see, for example, this great plain to the north here with those bright green spots scattered thickly over it?"

"Yes, they seem more fertile than the rest."
Stapleton laughed.

"That is the great GRIMPEN MIRE," said
he. "A false step yonder means death to man or
beast. Even in dry seasons it is a danger to cross
it, but after these autumn rains it is an awful
place. And yet I can find my way to the very
heart of it and return alive. There are one or two
paths which a very active man can take. I have
found them out."

GRIMPEN MIRE
V. dangerous
Do not enter
Keep dogs on lead

"But why should you wish to go into so horrible a place?"

"Well, you see the hills beyond? That is where the rare plants and the butterflies are."

"I shall try my luck some day –

HOOOOOOOOOOOOOOO

OOOOOOOOOOO

HALLOA!

OOO

OWL!

I cried.

What is that?

A long, low moan, indescribably sad, swept over the moor. From a dull murmur it swelled into a deep roar, and then sank back into a melancholy, throbbing murmur once again

Stapleton looked at me with a curious expression in his face.

They say it is the **HOUND OF THE BASKERVILLES** calling for its prey.

I've heard it once or twice before, but never quite so loud.

I looked round, with a chill of fear in my heart.

Nothing stirred over the vast expanse save a pair of ravens, which croaked loudly from a tor behind us.

Croak!

You are an educated man. You don't believe such nonsense as that?

said I.

What do you think is the cause of so strange a sound?

"Bogs make queer noises sometimes.

| It's the mud settling, | or the water rising, | or something." |

"No, no, that was a living voice."

"Well, perhaps it was."

"It's the weirdest, strangest thing that ever I heard in my life."

"Yes, it's an uncanny place altogether . . . Oh, excuse me an instant! It is surely Cyclopides."

A small fly or moth had fluttered across our path,

← Cyclopides (a butterfly)

and in an instant Stapleton was rushing with extraordinary energy and speed in pursuit of it. His grey clothes and jerky, zigzag, irregular progress made him not unlike some huge moth himself. I was standing watching his pursuit when I heard the sound of steps, and turning round found a woman near me upon the path. I could not doubt that this was Miss Stapleton.

GO BACK! she said.

Go straight back to London, instantly.

I could only stare at her in stupid surprise.

Why should I go back? I asked.

"I cannot explain." She spoke in a low, eager voice. "Go back and NEVER SET FOOT UPON THE MOOR AGAIN."

"But I have only just come."

MAN, MAN! she cried.

Can you not tell when a warning is for your own good?

GO BACK TO LONDON!

Get away from this place at all costs!

Hush, my brother is coming!

Stapleton had abandoned the chase and came back to us breathing hard and flushed with his exertions.

"Halloa, Beryl!" said he. His small light eyes glanced incessantly from the girl to me. "You have introduced yourselves, I see."

Yes. I was telling Sir Henry that it was rather late for him to see the true beauties of the moor.

Oh! She thinks I'm Henry!!

"No, no," said I. "My name is Dr Watson."

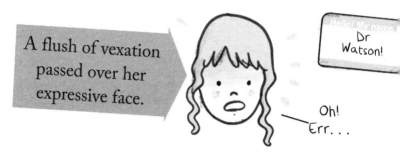

A flush of vexation passed over her expressive face.

Oh! Err...

"We have been talking at cross purposes," said she. "Dr Watson will you come and see Merripit House?"

A short walk brought us to it, a bleak moorland house. An orchard surrounded it, but the trees, as is usual upon the moor, were stunted and nipped, and the effect of the whole place was mean and melancholy.

"Queer spot to choose, is it not?" said he. "I had a school. It was in the north country. However, the fates were against us and the school closed.

Here we have books, we have our studies, and we have interesting neighbours. Do you think that I should intrude if I were to call this afternoon and make the acquaintance of Sir Henry?"

"I am sure that he would be delighted."

The melancholy of the moor, and the weird sound which had been associated with the grim legend of the Baskervilles, tinged my thoughts with sadness. Then there had come the definite and distinct warning of Miss Stapleton. I resisted all pressure to stay for lunch, and I set off at once upon my return journey, taking the grass-grown path by which we had come.

Before I had reached the road I was astounded to see Miss Stapleton sitting upon a rock by the side of the track.

I have run all the way in order to cut you off, Dr Watson,

said she.

If you have any influence with Sir Henry, take him away from a place which has always been fatal to his family.

I fear that unless you can give me some more definite information than this it would be impossible to get him to move.

"My brother is very anxious to have the Hall inhabited, for he thinks it is for the good of the poor folk upon the moor. He would be very angry if he knew that I have said anything which might induce Sir Henry to go away. GOOD-BYE!"

ITS A MYSTERY! MRS STAPLETON Why is she so keen that Henry doesn't stick around?

She turned and had disappeared in a few minutes among the scattered boulders, while I, with my soul full of vague fears, pursued my way to Baskerville Hall.

CHAPTER 7
FIRST REPORT OF
DR WATSON

GRIMPEN
Devon
POST OFFICE

Baskerville Hall,
October 13th.

MY DEAR HOLMES,

My previous letters and telegrams
have kept you pretty well up to date
as to all that has occurred in this most
God-forsaken corner of the world. The
longer one stays here the more does the
spirit of the moor sink into one's soul.

A very surprising circumstance occurred,
which I shall tell you in due course. But,
first of all, I must keep you in touch with
some of the other factors in the situation.

One of these is the escaped convict upon the moor. There is strong reason now to believe that he has got right away.

PRISON

Escapee

SELDEN

A very naughty boy

Of course, so far as his concealment goes there is no difficulty at all. Any one of the stone cottages would give him a hiding-place. But there is nothing to eat unless he were to catch and slaughter one of the moor sheep. We think, therefore, that he has gone.

Selden might be hiding in a stone cottage

He might be eating lots of lamb

I confess that I have had uneasy moments when I have thought of the Stapletons. The fact is that our friend, Sir Henry, begins to display a considerable interest in Miss Stapleton.

He like likes her! Uh oh . . .

BERYL

(Stapleton's sister)

There is something about her which forms a singular contrast to her cool and unemotional brother. There is a dry glitter in his eyes, and a firm set of his thin lips, which goes with a positive and possibly a harsh nature.

STAPLETON

Dry, glittery eyes

Generally quite harsh?

Firm lips

You would find him an interesting study.

He took us both to show us the spot where the legend of the wicked Hugo is supposed to have had its origin. It was an excursion of some miles across the moor which led to an open, grassy space.

In the middle rose two great stones, worn and sharpened at the upper end, until they looked like the huge corroding fangs of some monstrous beast . . .

By the way, your instructions to me never to allow Sir Henry to go out alone will become very much more onerous if a love affair were to be added to our other difficulties.

My popularity would soon suffer.

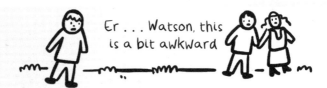

Er . . . Watson, this is a bit awkward

The other day – Thursday – Dr Mortimer lunched with us. The Stapletons came in afterwards, and the good doctor took us all to the Yew Alley, at Sir Henry's request, to show us exactly how everything occurred upon that fatal night.

And this is the Yew Alley

I remembered your theory of the affair and tried to picture all that had occurred. The old man saw something coming across the moor, something which terrified him so that he lost his wits, and ran and ran until he died of sheer horror and exhaustion.

And from what?

A sheep-dog of the moor?

Or a spectral hound,
black, silent, and monstrous?

One other neighbour I have met since I wrote last. This is MR FRANKLAND, of Lafter Hall. He is an elderly man, red-faced, white-haired, and choleric.

Super old →

← Old hair

Tomato face →

← Grumpy

His passion is for the British law. He fights for the mere pleasure of fighting and is equally ready to take up either side of a question. Being an amateur astronomer, he has an excellent telescope, with which he lies upon the roof of his own house and sweeps the moor all day in the hope of catching a glimpse of the escaped convict.

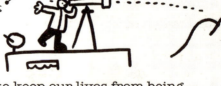

Mr Frankland's excellent telescope

He helps to keep our lives from being monotonous and gives a little comic relief where it is badly needed.

Let me end on that which is most
important and tell you more about the
BARRYMORES, and especially about the
surprising development of last night.

First of all about the test telegram, which
you sent from London in order to make sure
that Barrymore was really here. Sir Henry,
in his downright fashion, asked Barrymore
whether he had received the telegram
himself. Barrymore said that he had.

I did get it!
I promise I was here
the whole time!

Are you calling
me a liar??

Sir Henry had to pacify him by giving him
a considerable part of his old wardrobe,
the London outfit having now all arrived.

All right, all right!
Here . . . . have
my old clothes

Ooh,
thanks!

Boots

Shirt

A Hat

Mrs Barrymore is of interest to me. I have more than once observed traces of tears upon her face.

Some deep sorrow gnaws ever at her heart.

Last night, about two in the morning, I was aroused by a stealthy step passing my room. A long black shadow was trailing down the corridor. I could merely see the outline, but his height told me that it was Barrymore.

I could see from the glimmer of light through an open door that he had entered one of the rooms. I crept down the passage as noiselessly as I could and peeped round the corner of the door.

Barrymore was crouching at the window with the candle held against the glass. For some minutes he stood watching intently.

Then he gave a deep groan and with an impatient gesture he put out the light. Instantly I made my way back to my room, and very shortly came the stealthy steps passing once more upon their return journey.

There is some secret business going on in this house of gloom which sooner or later we shall get to the bottom of . . .

IT'S A MYSTERY!
THE
__BARRYMORES__
What are the Barrymores up to at night?

☐ ☐ ☐ *A letter from the desk of* ☐ ☐ ☐

John H. Watson, M.D.

...e of Sherlock Holmes, 'The Great Detective'

CHAPTER

8

THE LIGHT
UPON THE MOOR
[SECOND REPORT OF DR WATSON]

BASKERVILLE HALL,
Oct. 15th.

MY DEAR HOLMES –

Events are now crowding thick and fast
upon us. Things have taken a turn which
I could not have anticipated. But I will tell
you all and you shall judge for yourself.

On the morning following my adventure I went
down the corridor and examined the room in
which Barrymore had been on the night before.

This is where he was standing last night

The window commands the nearest outlook on the moor. Therefore Barrymore must have been looking out for something or somebody upon the moor.

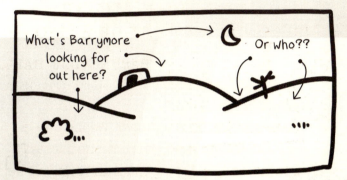

After breakfast I told Sir Henry all that I had seen. He was less surprised than I had expected.

"I knew that Barrymore walked about nights, and I had a mind to speak to him about it," said he.

"Two or three times I have heard his steps in the passage, coming and going, just about the hour you name."

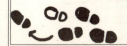

"Perhaps then he pays a visit every night to that particular window," I suggested. "Perhaps he does. I wonder what your friend Holmes would do, if he were here."

(You!)

"He would follow Barrymore and see what he did."
"Then we shall do it together. We'll sit up in my room tonight and wait until he passes."

***

After the conversation about Barrymore, Sir Henry put on his hat and prepared to go out. I did the same.

Right, I'm going out

OK I'll get my hat too

"What, are you coming, Watson?"

he asked, looking at me in a curious way.

AWKWARD!

"That depends on whether you are going on the moor," said I.

"Yes, I am."

"Well, you know what my instructions are. I am sorry to intrude, but you heard how earnestly Holmes insisted that you should not go alone upon the moor."

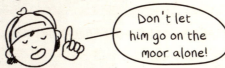

Don't let him go on the moor alone!

Sir Henry put his hand upon my shoulder with a pleasant smile.

Pleasant smile

Cheeky wink

"My dear fellow," said he, "I am sure that you are the last man in the world who would wish to be a spoilsport. I must go out alone."

It put me in a most awkward position. Before I had made up my mind he picked up his cane and was gone.

Err...

My conscience reproached me bitterly.
I imagined what my feelings would be if
some misfortune had occurred through
my disregard for your instructions . . .

I thought it might not be too late to
overtake him, so I set off at once in
the direction of Merripit House.

I hurried along the road until I came to
the point where the moor path branches
off. There, I mounted a hill and I saw him
at once. He was on the moor path, about a
quarter of a mile off, and a lady was by his
side who could only be Miss Stapleton.
They were walking slowly along
in deep conversation.

To act the spy upon a friend was a hateful task. Still, I could see no better course than to observe him from the hill.

Sir Henry and the lady had halted on the path when I was suddenly aware that I was not the only witness of their interview. A wisp of green floating in the air caught my eye. It was Stapleton with his butterfly net. He was running wildly towards them, his absurd net dangling behind him. He gesticulated and almost danced with excitement.

Finally Stapleton beckoned to his sister,
who, after a glance at Sir Henry, walked off
by the side of her brother. Sir Henry walked
slowly back the way that he had come, his
head hanging, the very picture of dejection.

I ran down the hill therefore and
met Sir Henry at the bottom.

"HALLOA, WATSON! Where
have you dropped from?" said he.

I explained how I had found it impossible to
remain behind, how I had followed him, and
how I had witnessed all that had occurred.
For an instant his eyes blazed at me, but he
broke at last into a rather rueful laugh.

Furious

ha

Laugh
(rueful)

"By thunder, the whole countryside seems to have been out to see me do my wooing – and a mighty poor wooing at that! Where had you engaged a seat?"

"I was on that hill."

"Quite in the back row, eh? But her brother was well up to the front. What's the matter with me, anyhow? Is there anything that would prevent me from making a good husband to a woman that I loved?"
"I should say not." said I.

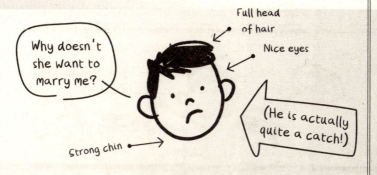

"I've only known her these few weeks, but from the first I just felt that she was made for me, and she, too – she was happy when she was with me, and that I'll swear.

"She was glad to meet me, but she kept coming back to it that this was a place of danger, and that she would never be happy until I had left it.

You're nice and all . . . . but you must leave this place!

Seriously, don't stick around

I GO!!!

"I told her that if she really wanted me to go, the only way to work it was for her to arrange to go with me. With that I offered in as many words to marry her, but before she could answer, down came this brother of hers, running at us with a face on him like a madman.

Oh brother. . .

"What was I doing with the lady?

"Did I think that because I was a BARONET I could do what I liked?

"I lost my temper too, and I answered him rather more hotly than I should perhaps.

"So it ended by his going off with her, as you saw, and here am I as badly puzzled a man as any in this county. Just tell me what it all means, Watson, and I'll owe you more than ever I can hope to pay."

🦋 🦋 🦋

Our conjectures were set at rest by a visit from Stapleton himself that afternoon. He had come to offer apologies for his rudeness of the morning, and after a long private interview with Sir Henry in his study, the breach is quite healed, and that we are to dine at Merripit House next Friday.

Friends again!

"I can't forget the look in his eyes when he ran at me this morning," said Sir Henry,

"but I must allow that no man could make a more handsome apology than he has done."

"Did he give any explanation of his conduct?"

"His sister is everything in his life, he says. They have always been together, and the thought of losing her was really terrible to him. He had not understood, he said, that I was becoming attached to her. It gave him such a shock that for a time he was not responsible for what he said or did. He was very sorry for all that had passed."

So there is one of our small mysteries cleared up.

 Watson xxx

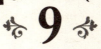

John H. Watson, M.D.

Associate of Sherlock Holmes, 'The Great Detective'

ANOTHER LETTER!

CHAPTER

9

(MORE FROM DR WATSON)

And now I pass on to the mystery of the SOBS IN THE NIGHT, of the tear-stained face of Mrs Barrymore, of the secret journey of the butler to the western window. All these things have by one night's work been thoroughly cleared.

I sat up with Sir Henry in his rooms until nearly three o'clock in the morning. It was incredible how slowly the hours crawled. One struck, and two, and we had almost given it up in despair, when we both sat bolt upright in our chairs.

We had heard the creak of a step in the passage.

That's him!

Sir Henry gently opened his door
and we set out in pursuit.

We had taken the precaution of leaving our
boots behind us, but, even so, the old boards
snapped and creaked beneath our tread . . .

We found Barrymore
crouching at the window,
candle in hand, his face
pressed against the pane,
exactly as I had seen
him the night before.

The baronet walked into the room, and as
he did so Barrymore sprang up from the
window. His dark eyes were full of HORROR
and ASTONISHMENT
as he gazed from
Sir Henry to me.

Horror!
Astonishment!!

"What are you doing here, Barrymore?" said Sir Henry.

"Nothing, sir." His agitation was so great that he could hardly speak, and the shadows sprang up and down from the shaking of his candle.

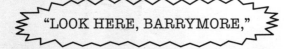

"LOOK HERE, BARRYMORE,"

said Sir Henry, sternly; "NO LIES! What were you doing at that window?"

The fellow wrung his hands together in misery.

"Don't ask me, Sir Henry – don't ask me! It is not my secret, and I cannot tell it."

I took the candle from the trembling hand of the butler.

"He must have been holding it as a signal," said I. I held it as he had done, and stared out into the darkness of the night. And then I gave a cry, for a tiny pin-point of yellow light had suddenly transfixed the dark veil, and glowed steadily in the centre of the black square framed by the window.

A tiny light, out on the moor

"There it is!" I cried.

"No, no, sir, it is nothing – nothing at all!" the butler broke in; "I assure you, sir –"

"Move your light across the window, Watson!" cried Sir Henry. "See, the other moves also! Now, you rascal, do you deny that it is a signal? What is this conspiracy that is going on?"

The man's face became openly defiant.

"I WILL NOT TELL."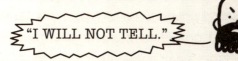

"Then you leave my employment right away." said Sir Henry. "By thunder, you may well be ashamed of yourself. Your family has lived with mine for over a hundred years under this roof, and here I find you deep in some dark plot against me."

"NO, NO, SIR; NO, NOT AGAINST YOU!"

It was a woman's voice, and Mrs Barrymore, paler and more horror-struck than her husband, was standing at the door.

"We have to go, Eliza. You can pack our things," said the butler.

This is all my fault!

"Oh, John, John, have I brought you to this? It is my doing, Sir Henry – all mine. He has done nothing except for my sake and because I asked him." she said.

"Speak out, then! What does it mean?"

"My unhappy brother is starving on the moor. We cannot let him perish at our very gates. The light is a signal to him that food is ready for him, and his light out yonder is to show the spot to which to bring it."

"Then your brother is –"

Whoa! →

"The escaped convict, sir – SELDEN, THE CRIMINAL."

SELDEN

Sir Henry and I both stared at her in AMAZEMENT.

IT'S A MYSTERY!
THE WEEPING WOMAN
Mrs Barrymore was crying for her brother, the escaped criminal!

MYSTERY SOLVED!

Was it possible that this respectable person was of the same blood as one of the most NOTORIOUS criminals in the country?

"Yes, sir, he is my younger brother. From crime to crime he sank lower and lower; but to me, sir, he was always the little curly-headed boy that I had nursed and played with, as an elder sister would.

Young Selden

"That was why he broke prison, sir. He knew that I was here and that we could not refuse to help him. We took him in and fed him and cared for him.

Here you go, bro

Thanks sis. Makes a nice change from prison porridge

Then you returned, sir, and my brother thought he would be safer on the moor. But every second night we made sure if he was still there by putting a light in the window, and if there was an answer my husband took out some bread and meat to him."

"Is this true, Barrymore?"

"Yes, Sir Henry. Every word of it."

"Well, I cannot blame you for standing by your own wife. Forget what I have said. Go to your room, you two, and we shall talk further about this matter in the morning."

When they were gone we looked out of the window again. Far away in the black distance there still glowed that one tiny point of yellow light.

"It cannot be far if Barrymore had to carry out the food," said Sir Henry. "And he is waiting, this villain, beside that candle.

By thunder, Watson, I AM GOING OUT TO TAKE THAT MAN!"

Jacket on – ready for ACTION!

The same thought had crossed my own mind. The man was a danger to the community. Any night, for example, our neighbours the Stapletons might be attacked by him, and it may have been the thought of this which made Sir Henry so keen upon the adventure.

"I will come," said I.

He loves Beryl Stapleton!

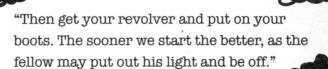

"Then get your revolver and put on your boots. The sooner we start the better, as the fellow may put out his light and be off."

In five minutes we were outside the door. We hurried through the dark shrubbery, amid the dull moaning of the autumn wind and the rustle of the falling leaves. Now and again the moon peeped out for an instant, but clouds were driving over the face of the sky, and just as we came out on the moor a thin rain began to fall. The light still burned steadily in front.

"I say, Watson," said the baronet, "what would Holmes say to this?"

John H. Watson, M.D.

Associate of Sherlock Holmes, 'The Great Detective'

HOOoWL! CHAPTER

ANOTHER LETTER!

❧ 10 ❧

HOWL!

(MORE FROM DR WATSON)

HOOooooOOOOOoOOoOOoOoOowL!

As if in answer to his words there rose
suddenly out of the vast gloom of the moor
that strange cry which I had already heard
upon the borders of the great Grimpen Mire.

HOWL!

HOoooooOOooooOowL!

It came with the wind through the silence of the
night, a long, deep mutter, then a rising howl,
and then the sad moan in which it died away.

HOoOoOOowL!

HOWL!

Again and again it sounded, the whole air
throbbing with it, strident, wild, and menacing.
The baronet caught my sleeve and his face
glimmered white through the darkness.

"My God, what's that, Watson?"

HOWL!

"I don't know. It's a sound they have on the moor. I heard it once before." It died away, and an absolute silence closed in upon us. We stood straining our ears, but nothing came.

"Watson," said the baronet, "it was the cry of a HOUND."

My blood ran cold in my veins, for there was a break in his voice which told of the sudden horror which had seized him.

"What do they call this sound?" he asked.

I hesitated but could not escape the question.

"They say it is the cry of the

He groaned and was silent for a few moments. "My God, can there be some truth in all these stories? Is it possible that I am really in danger from so dark a cause? You don't believe it, do you, Watson?"

"No, no."

"And yet it was one thing to laugh about it in London, and it is another to stand out here in the darkness of the moor and to hear such a cry as that.

"And my uncle! There was the footprint of the hound beside him as he lay. It all fits together. I don't think that I am a coward, Watson, but that sound seemed to freeze my very blood.

Feel my hand!"

It was as cold as a block of marble.

"Shall we turn back?"

"No, by thunder; we have come out to get our man, and we will do it."

We stumbled slowly along in the darkness, with the black loom of the craggy hills around us, and the yellow speck of light burning steadily in front.

That tiny light, again

There is nothing so deceptive as the distance of a light upon a pitch-dark night. But at last we knew that we were indeed very close. A guttering candle was stuck in a crevice of the rocks. It was strange to see this single candle burning there in the middle of the moor, with no sign of life near it.

"What shall we do now?"
whispered Sir Henry.

"Let us see if we can get a glimpse of him."
The words were hardly out of my
mouth when we both saw him.

AN EVIL FACE,

a TERRIBLE
animal
face,

FOUL
with
mire,

with a
BRISTLING
BEARD,
and hung
with MATTED
HAIR.

Any instant he might dash out the light and vanish in the darkness. I sprang forward therefore, and Sir Henry did the same. The man sprang to his feet and turned to run.

At the same moment by a lucky chance the moon broke through the clouds.

We rushed over the brow of the hill, and there was our man, springing over the stones in his way with the activity of a mountain goat.

He's getting away!

We were both swift runners and in fairly good training, but we had no chance of overtaking him. We saw him for a long time in the moonlight until he was only a small speck moving swiftly among the boulders upon the side of a distant hill.

He's definitely getting away!

There he goes!

Finally we stopped and sat panting on two rocks, while we watched him disappearing in the distance.

He got away!

Huff!

Puff!

Pant

Wheeze

And it was at this moment that there occurred a most STRANGE and UNEXPECTED thing. We were turning to go home, having abandoned the hopeless chase.

Who the heck?!?

The moon was low upon the right, and there, outlined as black as an ebony statue, I saw the figure of a MAN UPON THE TOR.

As far as I could judge, the figure was that of a tall, thin man.

He stood with his legs a little separated, his arms folded, his head bowed. It was not the convict. With a cry of surprise I pointed him out to Sir Henry, but the man was gone.

LOOK! There's someone up there – but who!?

Such are the adventures of last night, and you must acknowledge, my dear Holmes, that I have done you very well in the matter of a report.

So far as the Barrymores go we have found the motive of their actions.

But the moor remains as inscrutable as ever. Best of all would it be if you could come down to us. In any case you will hear from me again in the next few days.

Watson xoxo

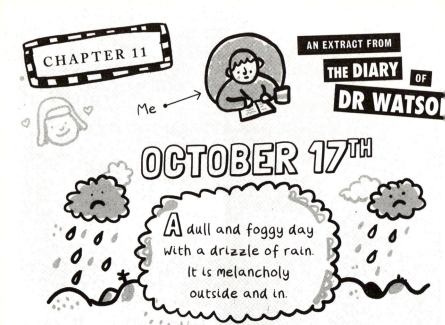

CHAPTER 11

Me →

OCTOBER 17TH

A dull and foggy day
with a drizzle of rain.
It is melancholy
outside and in.

Sir Henry is in a black reaction after the excitements of the night. I am conscious myself of a feeling of ever present danger, which is the more terrible because I am unable to define it. And have I not cause for such a feeling?

There is the **DEATH** of the last occupant of the Hall, fulfilling so exactly the conditions of the FAMILY LEGEND, and there are the repeated reports of the appearance of a strange creature upon the moor. TWICE I have with my own ears heard the sound which resembled the DISTANT BAYING OF A HOUND.

THE FAMILY LEGEND

WOOF! Woof!

A spectral hound which leaves FOOTMARKS and fills the air with its **HOWLING** is surely not to be thought of.

If I have one quality upon earth it is common-sense, and NOTHING will persuade me to believe in such a thing. But FACTS ARE FACTS, and I have TWICE heard this crying upon the moor.

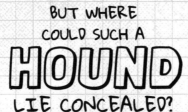

BUT WHERE COULD SUCH A **HOUND** LIE CONCEALED?

AND ALWAYS, APART FROM THE HOUND,

there is the **MAN IN THE CAB**,

and the **LETTER** which warned Sir Henry against the moor.

Where is that friend or enemy now?

Could he be the **STRANGER** whom I saw upon the tor?

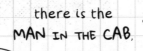

IT IS TRUE THAT I HAVE HAD ONLY THE ONE GLANCE AT HIM, and yet there are some things to which I am ready to swear.

HE IS NO ONE WHOM I HAVE SEEN DOWN HERE, and I have now met ALL the neighbours.

The figure was far taller than that of Stapleton, far thinner than that of Frankland.

Barrymore it might possibly have been, but I am certain that he could not have followed us.

A STRANGER THEN IS STILL DOGGING US.

IT'S A MYSTERY!
THE MAN ON THE TOR
Who is he ... and what does he want??

WE HAD A SMALL SCENE THIS MORNING AFTER BREAKFAST.

Barrymore asked to speak with Sir Henry in his study. After a time the baronet called for me.

Barrymore thinks that it was unfair on our part to hunt his brother-in-law down when he had told us the secret.

The butler was standing very pale but very collected before us.

"I didn't think you would have taken advantage of it, Sir Henry - indeed I didn't." said Barrymore.

"The man is a **PUBLIC DANGER**. There's no safety for anyone until he is under lock and key," said Sir Henry.

I assure you, Sir Henry, that in a very few days the necessary arrangements will have been made and he will be on his way to South America. You can't tell on him without getting my wife and me into trouble. **I BEG YOU**, sir, to say nothing to the police.

 What do you say, Watson?

I shrugged my shoulders.

 If he were safely out of the country it would relieve the taxpayer of a burden.

"That is true," said Sir Henry. "Well, Barrymore –"

"GOD BLESS YOU, SIR! It would have killed my poor wife had he been taken again."

"I guess we are aiding and abetting a felony, Watson? All right, Barrymore, you can go."

The man turned, but then came back.

 You've been so kind to us, sir, that I should like to do the best I can for you in return. I know something, Sir Henry. It's about poor Sir Charles's death.

SIR HENRY AND I WERE BOTH UPON OUR FEET.

 "DO YOU KNOW HOW HE DIED?"

 No, sir, I don't know that.

What then?

I know why he was at the gate at that hour. It was **TO MEET A WOMAN**.

"How do you know this, Barrymore?"

Well, Sir Henry, your uncle had a letter that morning. It was from Coombe Tracey, and it was addressed in a <u>WOMAN'S HAND</u>.

"I thought no more of the matter, and never would have done had it not been for my wife. Only a few weeks ago she was cleaning out Sir Charles's study – it had never been touched since his death – and she found the ashes of a burned letter in the back of the grate.

"The greater part of it was charred to pieces, but the end of a page hung together, and the writing could still be read. It said:

Please, please, as you are a gentleman, burn this letter, and be at the gate by ten o'clock. *L. L.*

Beneath it were signed the initials L. L.

IT'S A MYSTERY!
THE LETTER
Who was this L. L. who sent Sir Henry a letter? Lindsay Lohan? Leona Lewis!! And what did it say?

"And you have no idea who L. L. is?"

"No, sir. No more than you have."

"Very good, Barrymore; you can go."

WHEN THE BUTLER HAD LEFT US SIR HENRY TURNED TO ME.

Well, Watson, what do you think of this new light?

It seems to leave the darkness rather blacker than before.

So I think. But if we can only trace L. L. it should clear up the whole business.

I went at once to my room and drew up my report of the morning's conversation for HOLMES. It was evident to me that he had been very busy of late.

I WISH THAT HE WERE HERE.

OCTOBER 17TH

All day today the rain poured down, rustling on the ivy and dripping from the eaves. In the evening I put on my waterproof and I walked far upon the sodden moor, full of dark imaginings.

I found the black tor upon which I had seen the solitary watcher, and from its craggy summit I looked out myself across the melancholy downs.

In the distant hollow on the left, the two thin towers of Baskerville Hall rose above the trees.

Nowhere was there any trace of that lonely man whom I had seen on the same spot two nights before.

As I walked back I was overtaken by **DR MORTIMER**. He insisted upon my climbing into his dog-cart, and he gave me a lift homeward.

"By the way, Mortimer," said I as we jolted along the rough road, "Can you tell me the name of any woman whose initials are L. L.?"

He thought for a few minutes.

There is **LAURA LYONS** - her initials are L. L. - but she lives in Coombe Tracey.

"Who is she?" I asked.

She is Frankland's daughter.

WHAT! OLD FRANKLAND THE CRANK?

IT'S A MYSTERY!
THE LETTER
It might have been sent by a lady called Laura Lyons, daughter of Frankland

"Exactly. She married an **ARTIST** named Lyons, who came sketching on the moor. He proved to be a scoundrel and deserted her. So the girl has had a pretty bad time."

"How does she live?"

"Her story got about, and several of the people here did something to enable her to earn a living. It was to set her up in a typewriting business."

I HAVE ONLY ONE OTHER INCIDENT TO RECORD.

This was my conversation with Barrymore just now.

Mortimer had stayed to dinner, and he and Sir Henry played ecarté afterwards. The butler brought me my coffee into the library, and I took the chance to ask him a few questions.

Well has this precious relation of yours departed, or is he still LURKING out yonder?

I don't know, sir. I've not heard of him since I left out food for him last, and that was three days ago.

Did you see him then?

No, sir, but the food was gone when next I went that way.

Then he was certainly there?

So you would think, sir,

unless it was the **OTHER MAN** who took it.

I sat with my coffee-cup halfway to my lips and STARED at Barrymore.

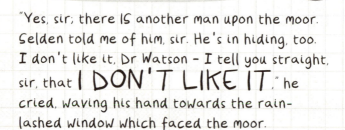

YOU KNOW THAT THERE IS ANOTHER MAN THEN?

"Yes, sir; there IS another man upon the moor. Selden told me of him, sir. He's in hiding, too. I don't like it, Dr Watson – I tell you straight, sir, that I DON'T LIKE IT," he cried, waving his hand towards the rain-lashed window which faced the moor.

Can you tell me anything about this stranger? What did Selden say?

"He saw him once or twice. A kind of GENTLEMAN he was, as far as he could see, but what he was doing he could not make out."

"And where did he say that he lived?"

"Among the old houses on the hillside – the stone huts."

"But how about his food?"

"He has got a lad who works for him and brings him all he needs."

WHEN THE BUTLER
HAD GONE I WALKED OVER
TO THE BLACK WINDOW.

There, in that hut upon the moor, seems to lie the very centre of that problem which has vexed me so sorely.

I swear that another day shall not have passed before I have done all that man can do to reach the heart of the mystery.

THE NEXT DAY I drove off upon my new quest to find Mrs Lyons.

When I reached Coombe Tracey I had no difficulty in finding her rooms. As I entered the sitting-room a lady sprang up with a pleasant smile of welcome. Her eyes and hair were of the same rich hazel colour, and her cheeks were flushed.

Hello there!

It was about the late Sir Charles Baskerville that I have come here to see you,

said I.

The freckles started out on the lady's face.

I owe a great deal to his kindness.

"Did you write to Sir Charles asking him to meet you on the very day of Sir Charles's death?"

I thought that she had fainted, but she recovered herself by a supreme effort.

"I have no reason to be ashamed of it. I wished him to help me."

"What happened when you did get there?"

"I never went."

IT'S A MYSTERY!
THE LETTER
It was sent by Laura Lyons! But why??

MRS LYONS!

No, I swear it to you on all I hold sacred. I never went.

The matter is a very private one.

It was unlikely that she would say that she had not been to Baskerville Hall if she really had been. Such an excursion could not be kept secret. I came away baffled and disheartened. And yet I felt that something was being held back from me . . .

For now I must turn back to that other clue among the stone huts upon the moor.

I should explore every hut upon the moor until I lighted upon the right one. If this man were inside it I should find out from his own lips who he was and why he had dogged us so long. Holmes had missed him in London. It would indeed be a triumph for me if I could run him to earth, where my master had failed.

Luck had been against us again and again in this inquiry, but now at last it came to my aid. And the messenger of good fortune was none other than Mr Frankland, who was standing, grey-whiskered and red-faced, outside the gate of his garden.

GOOD-DAY, DR WATSON, cried he,

you must really give your horses a rest, and come in to have a glass of wine.

I wouldn't say no to a cheeky Sauvignon Blanc

I alighted and sent a message to Sir Henry that I should walk over in time for dinner. Then I followed Frankland into his dining-room.

"It is one of the red-letter days of my life," he cried with many chuckles. "Already my words have come true."

"How so?" I asked.

The old man put on a very knowing expression.

Some poaching case, no doubt? said I.

Ha, ha, my boy, a very much more important matter than that!

The Devonshire Daily
NOTTING HILL MURDERER STILL ON THE LOOSE

What about the CONVICT ON THE MOOR?

I stared. "You don't mean that you know where he is?" said I.

I may not know exactly where he is, but I have seen with my own eyes the child who takes him his food.

I see him every day through my telescope upon the roof.

He passes along the same path at the same hour, and to whom should he be going except to the convict?

Here was luck indeed! A child! Barrymore had said that our unknown man on the moor was supplied by a boy. It was on his track, and not upon the convict's, that Frankland had stumbled.

"I have seen the boy again and again with his bundle. Every day, and sometimes twice a day, I have been able – but wait a moment, Dr Watson. Do my eyes deceive me, or is there something moving upon that hillside?"

It was several miles off, but I could distinctly see a small dark dot against the dull green and grey.

"Come, sir, come!" cried Frankland, rushing upstairs. "You will see with your own eyes and judge for yourself."

The telescope, a formidable instrument mounted upon a tripod, stood upon the flat leads of the house. Frankland clapped his eye to it and gave a cry of satisfaction.

Quick, Dr Watson, quick, before he passes over the hill!

There he was, sure enough, a small urchin with a little bundle upon his shoulder, toiling slowly up the hill.

He looked round him with a furtive and stealthy air, as one who dreads pursuit.

13

A SECRET WITHIN
MY GRASP

I SUCCEEDED IN DISSUADING Frankland from walking home with me. I kept the road as long as his eye was on me, and then I struck off across the moor and made for the stony hill over which the boy had disappeared.

The sun was already sinking when I reached the summit of the hill, and the long slopes beneath me were all golden-green on one side and grey shadow on the other.

The boy was nowhere to be seen. But down beneath me in a cleft of the hills there was a circle of the old stone huts, and in the middle of them there was one which retained sufficient roof to act as a screen against the weather.

My heart leaped within me as I saw it.

This must be the burrow where the stranger lurked.

His secret was within my grasp.

As I approached the hut, walking as warily as Stapleton would do when he drew near a settled butterfly, net poised, I satisfied myself that the place had indeed been used as a habitation.

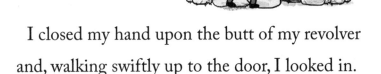

I closed my hand upon the butt of my revolver and, walking swiftly up to the door, I looked in.

The place was empty.

But there were ample signs that I had not come upon a false scent. This was certainly where the man lived.

Some blankets rolled in a waterproof lay upon that very stone slab upon which Neolithic man had once slumbered.

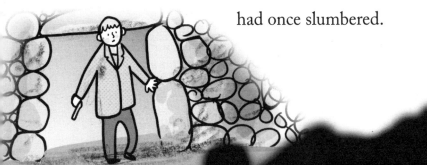

The ashes of a fire were heaped in a rude grate.

Beside it lay some cooking utensils

and a bucket half-full of water.

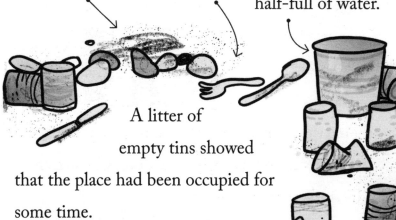

A litter of empty tins showed that the place had been occupied for some time.

In the middle of the hut stood a small cloth bundle – the same, no doubt, which I had seen through the telescope upon the shoulder of the boy. It contained a loaf of bread, a tinned tongue, and two tins of preserved peaches.

My heart leaped to see that beneath it there lay a sheet of paper with writing upon it.

This was what I read, roughly scrawled in pencil:

Dr Watson has gone to Coombe Tracey.

It was I, then, and not Sir Henry, who was being dogged by this secret man. Always there was this feeling of an unseen force, a fine net drawn round us with infinite skill and delicacy. Was he our malignant enemy, or our guardian angel? I swore that I would not leave the hut until I knew.

IT'S A MYSTERY!
THE MAN ON
THE TOR
He's been watching Watson this whole time! But why ... and is he dangerous??

Outside the sun was sinking low and the west was blazing with scarlet and gold. With tingling nerves, but a fixed purpose, I sat in the dark recess of the hut and waited with sombre patience for the coming of its tenant.

And then at last I heard him. Far away came
the sharp clink of a boot striking upon a stone.
Then another
            and yet another,
                        coming nearer and nearer.

I shrank back into
the darkest corner, and
cocked the pistol in my
pocket, determined not
to discover myself until
I had an opportunity of
seeing something of the
stranger.

There was a long pause which showed that
he had stopped. Then once more the footsteps
approached and a shadow fell across the opening
of the hut.

It is a lovely evening, my dear Watson,

said a well-known voice.

I really think that you will be more comfortable outside than in.

14

DEATH *on the* MOOR

FOR A MOMENT or two I sat breathless, hardly able to believe my ears. That cold, incisive, ironical voice could belong to but one man in all the world.

HOLMES!

I cried –

HOLMES!

Come out,

said he,

and please be careful with the revolver.

There he sat upon a stone outside, his grey eyes dancing with amusement. He was thin and worn, but clear and alert, his keen face bronzed by the sun and roughened by the wind. In his tweed suit and cloth cap he looked like any other tourist upon the moor.

I never was more glad to see anyone in my life, said I, as I wrung him by the hand.

So you actually thought that I was the criminal?

I did not know who you were, but I was determined to find out.

Back on goes the hat!

"Excellent, Watson! And how did you localise me? You saw me, perhaps, on the night of the convict hunt, when I was so imprudent as to allow the moon to rise behind me?"

"Yes, I saw you then."

"And have no doubt searched all the huts until you came to this one?"

"No, your boy had been observed."

IT'S A MYSTERY!
THE MAN ON THE TOR
It was Sherlock flippin' Holmes!

MYSTERY SOLVED!

"The old gentleman with the telescope, no doubt. I could not make it out when first I saw the light flashing upon the lens."

He rose and peeped into the hut. "Ha, I see that Cartwright has brought up some supplies. What's this paper?

The helpful lad was Cartwright, the District Messenger!

"So you have been to Coombe Tracey, to see Mrs Laura Lyons?"

Dr Watson has gone to Coombe Tracey.

"Exactly. But how in the name of wonder did you come here, and what have you been doing? I thought that you were in Baker Street."

That as what **I WISHED you** to think.

"Then you use me, and yet do not trust me!" I cried with some bitterness.

"My dear fellow, you have been invaluable to me in this as in many other cases, and I beg that you will forgive me if I have seemed to play a trick upon you. Had I been with Sir Henry and you, my presence would have warned our very formidable opponents to be on their guard."

"But why keep me in the dark?"

"You would have wished to tell me something, or in your kindness you would have brought me out some comfort or other, and so an unnecessary risk would be run."

Then my reports have all been wasted!

Tap! Tap! Tap!

They took me ages!

My voice trembled as I recalled the pains and the pride with which I had composed them.

Holmes took a bundle of papers from his pocket.

Here are your reports, my dear fellow, and very well thumbed, I assure you.

I must compliment you exceedingly upon the zeal and the intelligence which you have shown over an extraordinarily difficult case.

The warmth of Holmes's praise drove my anger from my mind. I felt also in my heart that he was right in what he said and that it was really best for our purpose that I should not have known that he was upon the moor.

"That's better," said he, seeing the shadow rise from my face. "And now tell me the result of your visit to Mrs Laura Lyons."

The sun had set and dusk was settling over the moor. The air had turned chill and we withdrew into the hut for warmth. There, sitting together in the twilight, I told Holmes of my conversation with the lady.

"This is most important," said he when I had concluded. "It fills up a gap which I had been unable to bridge. You are aware, perhaps, that a close intimacy exists between Mrs Lyons and the man Stapleton?"

"I did not know of a close intimacy."

"There can be no doubt about the matter. They meet, they write, there is a complete understanding between them. Now, this puts a very powerful weapon into our hands. If I could only use it to detach his wife –"

"His wife?"

"The lady who has passed here as Stapleton's sister is in reality his wife."

BIG REVEALS!

Stapleton and Mrs Lyons are in love!?

Stapleton's sister is actually his wife!!!

"But why this elaborate deception?"

"Because she would be very much more useful to him."

All my unspoken instincts, my vague suspicions, suddenly took shape and centred upon the naturalist. In that impassive, colourless man, with his straw hat and his butterfly-net, I seemed to see something terrible – a creature of infinite patience and craft, with a smiling face and a murderous heart.

"It is he, then, who is our enemy – it is he who dogged us in London?"

"So I read the riddle."

"And the warning – it must have come from her!"

"Exactly."

"But are you sure of this, Holmes? How do you know that the woman is his wife?"

"Because he so far forgot himself as to tell you a true piece of autobiography upon the occasion when he first met you. He was once a schoolmaster in the north of England.

IT'S A MYSTERY!
THE MAN IN THE CAB
It was Stapleton!

MYSTERY SOLVED!

IT'S A MYSTERY!
THE WARNING
Was sent by Stapleton's sister, er . . . I mean wife!

MYSTERY SOLVED!

Stapleton mentioned this on p114!

Now, there is no one more easy to trace than a schoolmaster. A little investigation showed me that a school had come to grief under atrocious circumstances, and that the man who had owned it – the name was different – had disappeared with his wife. The descriptions agreed. When I learned that the missing man was devoted to entomology the identification was complete."

ENTOMOLOGY
The study of bugs and stuff.

Northern News

DAILY NEWS   FREE

SCHOOL'S OUT
. . . FOREVER

Local school closed.
A school in the north of England has had to close down after some atrocious events. The man who ran the school Mr Vandeleur, has now disappeared with his

CLOSED

wife Mrs Vandeleur. The missing man

was devoted to entomology.

The darkness was rising, but much was still hidden by the shadows.

❧198❧

"If this woman is in truth his wife, where does Mrs Laura Lyons come in?" I asked.

"Regarding Stapleton as an unmarried man, she counted no doubt upon becoming his wife. It must be our first duty to see her – both of us – tomorrow."

IT'S A MYSTERY!
__THE LETTER__
Laura Lyons was probably told to send it by Stapleton

The last red streaks had faded away in the west and night had settled upon the moor. A few faint stars were gleaming in a violet sky.

"One last question, Holmes," I said, as I rose. "What is the meaning of it all? What is he after?"

Holmes's voice sank as he answered:

IT IS **MURDER,** WATSON –

refined, cold-blooded, deliberate murder.

"My nets are closing upon him, even as his are upon Sir Henry, and with your help he is already almost at my mercy. There is but one danger which can threaten us. It is that he should strike before we are ready to do so. Another day – two at the most – and I have my case complete –

"HARK!"

AAAAAAAAAAAIIEE!!!

A terrible scream – a prolonged yell of horror and anguish – burst out of the silence of the moor.

That frightful cry turned the blood to ice in my veins.

15

LURKING AMONG THE ROCKS

HOLMES HAD SPRUNG to his feet, and I saw his dark, athletic outline at the door of the hut.

 Hush! he whispered.

 *Hush!*

The cry had pealed out from somewhere far off on the shadowy plain. Now it burst upon our ears, nearer, louder, more urgent than before.

Where is it? Holmes whispered; and I knew from the thrill of his voice that he, the man of iron, was shaken to the soul.

Where is it, Watson?

There, I think. I pointed into the darkness.

No, there!

Again the agonised cry swept through the silent night, louder and much nearer than ever. And a new sound mingled with it, a deep, muttered RUMBLE, musical and yet menacing, rising and falling like the low, constant murmur of the sea.

THE HOUND! cried Holmes.

Come, Watson, come! Great heavens, if we are too late!

He had started running swiftly over the moor, and I had followed at his heels.

But now from somewhere among the broken ground immediately in front of us there came one last despairing yell,

AAAAAAAAA AAAAAH!

THUD.

and then a dull, heavy thud.

WE HALTED AND LISTENED.

Not another sound broke the heavy silence of the windless night.

I saw Holmes put his hand to his forehead like a man distracted. He stamped his feet upon the ground.

He has beaten us, Watson.

We are too late.

No, no, surely not!

Blindly we ran through the gloom, blundering against boulders, forcing our way through gorse bushes, panting up hills and rushing down slopes, heading always in the direction whence those dreadful sounds had come.

"Can you see anything?"

"Nothing."

"But, hark, what is that?"

A low moan had fallen upon our ears.

There it was again upon our left! On that side a ridge of rocks ended in a sheer cliff. On its jagged face was spread-eagled some dark, irregular object. It was a prostrate man face downward upon the ground, the body hunched together as if in the act of throwing a somersault.

Holmes laid his hand upon him, and held it up again, with an exclamation of horror.

The gleam of the match which he struck shone upon his clotted fingers and upon the ghastly pool of blood.

And it shone upon something else which turned our hearts sick and faint within us –

THE BODY OF SIR HENRY BASKERVILLE!

There was no chance of either of us forgetting that peculiar ruddy tweed suit – the very one which he had worn on the first morning that we had seen him in Baker Street. We caught the one clear glimpse of it, and then the match flickered and went out, even as the hope had gone out of our souls. Holmes groaned, and his face glimmered white through the darkness.

THE BRUTE! THE BRUTE!

I cried with clenched hands.

Oh Holmes, I shall never forgive myself for having left him to his fate.

We stood with bitter hearts on either side of the mangled body, overwhelmed by this sudden and irrevocable disaster. The agony of those contorted limbs struck me with a spasm of pain.

and blurred my

eyes with tears.

WE MUST SEND FOR HELP, HOLMES!

We cannot carry him all the way to the Hall. Good heavens, are you mad?

Holmes had uttered a cry and bent over the body.

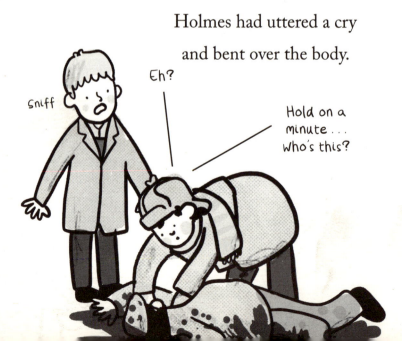

Sniff

Eh?

Hold on a minute . . . Who's this?

Now he was dancing and laughing and wringing my hand.

A **BEARD!** A BEARD!

Haha!

The man has a beard!

It is not Sir Henry – it is – why, it is the convict!

With feverish haste we had turned the body over, and that dripping beard was pointing up to the cold, clear moon. There could be no doubt about the beetling forehead, the sunken animal eyes.

It was indeed the same face which had glared upon me in the light of the candle from over the rock – the face of Selden, the criminal.

THEN IN AN INSTANT IT WAS ALL CLEAR TO ME.

I remembered how Sir Henry had told me that he had handed his old wardrobe to Barrymore. Barrymore had passed it on in order to help Selden in his escape. Boots, shirt, cap – it was all Sir Henry's. I told Holmes how the matter stood, my heart bubbling over with thankfulness and joy.

"Then the clothes have been the poor devil's death," said he. "It is clear enough that the hound has been given the scent of some article of Sir Henry's – the boot in the hotel, in all probability. The question now is, what shall we do with this poor wretch's body? We cannot leave

IT'S A MYSTERY!
THE BOOT
So the boot was used to give a scent of SIR HENRY to the hound!

MYSTERY SOLVED!

it here to the foxes and the ravens."

"I suggest that we put it in one of the huts until we can communicate with the police." said I.

"Exactly. I have no doubt that you and I could carry it so far. Halloa, Watson, what's this? IT'S THE MAN HIMSELF! Not a word to show your suspicions – not a word, or my plans crumble to the ground."

A figure was approaching us over the moor. The moon shone upon him, and I could distinguish the jaunty walk of the naturalist. He stopped when he saw us, and then came on again.

Why, Dr Watson, that's not you, is it?

It is me, Stapleton. And my colleague Sherlock Holmes, too!

You are the last man that I should have expected to see out on the moor at this time of night.

Not – don't tell me that it is our friend Sir Henry!

But, dear me, what's this? Somebody hurt?

Nice acting, Stapleton!

He hurried past me and stooped over the dead man. I heard a sharp intake of his breath.

Gasp!

Who – who's this?

he stammered.

It is Selden, the man who escaped from Princetown.

Stapleton turned a ghastly face upon us, but by a supreme effort he had overcome his amazement and his disappointment. He looked sharply from Holmes to me.

Dear me! What a very shocking affair!

How did he die?

"He appears to have broken his neck by falling over these rocks," said I. "My friend and I were strolling on the moor when we heard a cry."

"I heard a cry also. That was what brought me out. I was uneasy about Sir Henry."

"Why about Sir Henry in particular?" I could not help asking.

"Because I had suggested that he should come over. When he did not come I was surprised, and

I naturally became alarmed for his safety when I heard cries upon the moor. By the way" – his eyes darted again from my face to Holmes's – "did you hear anything else besides a cry?"

"No," said Holmes; "did you?"

"No."

"What do you mean, then?"

Oh, you know the stories about a **PHANTOM HOUND**, and so on. It is said to be heard at night upon the moor. I was wondering if there were any evidence of such a sound tonight.

"We heard nothing of the kind," said I.

Stapleton gave a sigh which I took to indicate his relief. "I would suggest carrying this poor fellow to my house, but it would give my sister such a fright. I think that if we put something over his face he will be safe until morning."

And so it was arranged. Holmes and I set off to Baskerville Hall, leaving the naturalist to return alone. Looking back we saw the figure moving slowly away over the broad moor, and behind him that one black smudge on the silvered slope which showed where the man was lying who had come so horribly to his end.

CHAPTER
❧ 16 ❧
THE MISSING LINK

"WE'RE AT CLOSE grips at last," said Holmes as we walked together across the moor.

I told you in London, Watson, and I tell you now again, that we have never had a foeman more worthy of our steel.

Why should we not arrest him at once?

said I.

"My dear Watson, you were born to be a man of action. Your instinct is always to do something energetic. But supposing, for argument's sake, that we had him arrested tonight, what on earth the better off should we be for that? We could prove nothing against him. There's the devilish cunning of it!"

"Surely we have a case."

"Not a shadow of one. We should be laughed out of court if we came with such a story and such evidence. No, my dear fellow; we must reconcile ourselves to the fact that we have no case at present, and that

it is worth our while to run any risk in order to establish one."

"And how do you propose to do so?"

"I have great hopes of what Mrs Laura Lyons may do for us when the position of affairs is made clear to her. And I have my own plan as well."

❦217❧

I could draw nothing further from him, and he walked, lost in thought, as far as the Baskerville gates.

"Yes; I see no reason for further concealment. But one last word, Watson. Say nothing of the hound to Sir Henry."

Sir Henry was more pleased than surprised to see Sherlock Holmes. He did raise his eyebrows, however, when he found that my friend had neither any luggage nor any explanations for its absence. Over a belated supper we explained to him as much of our experience as it seemed desirable that he should know. But first I had the unpleasant duty of breaking the news to Barrymore and his wife.

Sherlock and **I** were strolling on the moor when we heard a cry.

I'm sorry to say it was Selden, your brother. We arrived too late. He is dead,

To him it may have been an unmitigated relief, but she wept bitterly in her apron. To all the world the convict was the man of violence, half animal and half demon;

but to her

he always remained

the brother

who had clung

to her hand.

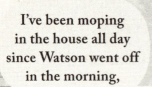

I've been moping in the house all day since Watson went off in the morning, said Sir Henry at supper.

If I hadn't sworn not to go about alone I might have had a more lively evening, for I had a message from Stapleton asking me over there.

I have no doubt that you would have had a more lively evening,

said Holmes drily.

Hey Sir Henry, Do you want to come over to our house tonight?
- Stapleton

"But how about the case?" asked Sir Henry. "Have you made anything out of the tangle?"

"It has been an exceedingly difficult and most complicated business. There are several points upon which we still want light – but it is coming all the same."

"We've had one experience, as Watson has no doubt told you," said Sir Henry. "We heard the hound on the moor. If you can muzzle him and put him on a chain I'll be ready to swear you are the greatest detective of all time."

"I think I will muzzle him and chain him all right if you will give me your help."

"Whatever you tell me to do I will do."

"If you will do this I think the chances are that our little problem will soon be solved. I have no doubt –"

Holmes stopped suddenly and stared fixedly up over my head into the air.

WHAT IS IT?

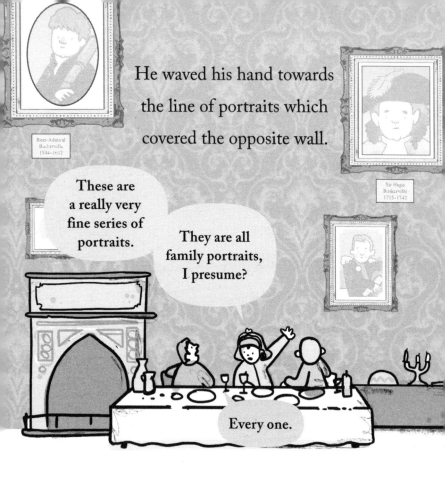

He waved his hand towards the line of portraits which covered the opposite wall.

These are a really very fine series of portraits.

They are all family portraits, I presume?

Every one.

"Who is the gentleman with the telescope?"

"That is Rear-Admiral Baskerville. The man with the blue coat and the roll of paper is Sir William Baskerville."

"And this Cavalier opposite to me – the one with the black velvet and the lace?"

"That is the cause of all the mischief, the wicked HUGO, who started the Hound of the Baskervilles. We're not likely to forget him."

I gazed with interest and some surprise upon the portrait.

"Dear me!" said Holmes. The picture of the old roysterer seemed to have a fascination for him, and his eyes were continually fixed upon it during supper.

Why is Sherlock so fascinated by this picture??

It was not until later, when Sir Henry had gone to his room, that I was able to follow the trend of his thoughts. He led me back into the banqueting hall, his bedroom candle in his hand, and he held it up against the time-stained portrait on the wall.

"Do you see anything there?" said Holmes.

I looked at the broad plumed hat, the curling love-locks, the white lace collar, and the severe fa which was framed between them.

It was not a brutal countenance, but it was prim, hard, and stern, with a firm-set, thin-lipped mouth, and a coldly intolerant eye.

"Is it like anyone you know?"

"There is something of Sir Henry about the jaw."

"Just a suggestion, perhaps. But wait an instant!" He stood upon a chair, and, holding up the light in his left hand, he curved his right arm over the broad hat and round the long ringlets.

GOOD HEAVENS!

I cried, in amazement.

The face of Stapleton had sprung out of the canvas.

"Ha, you see it now," said Holmes. "My eyes have been trained to examine faces and not their trimmings. It is the first quality of a criminal investigator that he should see through a disguise."

"But this is marvellous. It might be Stapleton's portrait."

"Yes. Stapleton is a Baskerville – that is evident. This picture has supplied us with one of our most obvious missing links. We have him, Watson, we have him, and I dare swear that before tomorrow night he will be fluttering in our net as helpless as one of his own butterflies."

IT'S A MYSTERY! WHY DID THEY DO IT? Stapleton is a Baskerville, and therefore a possible heir to Sir Charles's fortune.

CHAPTER
17
FIXING *the* NETS

He's up early!

I WAS UP BETIMES in the morning, but Holmes was afoot earlier still, for I saw him as I dressed, coming up the drive.

He rubbed his hands with the joy of action. "The nets are all in place!"

"What is the next move?"

"To see Sir Henry. Ah, here he is!"

"Good morning, Holmes," said Sir Henry. "You look like a general who is planning a battle."

"That is the exact situation. Watson was asking for orders."

"And so do I."

Very good. You are engaged, as I understand, to dine with our friends the Stapletons tonight?

I hope that you will come also. They are very hospitable people, and I am sure that they would be very glad to see you.

"I fear that Watson and I must go to London," said Holmes.

The baronet's face perceptibly lengthened.

Oh.

"When do you desire to go?"

"Immediately after breakfast. Watson, you will send a note to Stapleton to tell him that you regret that you cannot come for dinner."

I have a good mind to go to London with you,

Why should I stay here alone?

said Sir Henry.

"Because you gave me your word that you would do as you were told, and I tell you to stay."

"All right, then, I'll stay," said Sir Henry.

"One more direction! I wish you to drive to Merripit House. Send back your trap, however, and let Stapleton know that you intend to walk home."

To walk across the moor?

Yes.

But that is the VERY THING which you have so often cautioned me not to do.

It is essential that you should do it.

Go have dinner with the Stapletons

Tell them you plan to walk home across the moor – alone

Then I will do it.

We bade goodbye to our rueful friend, and a couple of hours afterwards we were at the station of Coombe Tracey. A small boy was waiting upon the platform with a telegram, which Holmes handed to me. It ran:

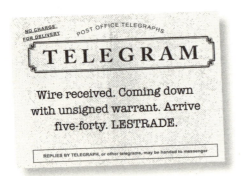

NO CHARGE FOR DELIVERY   POST OFFICE TELEGRAPHS

TELEGRAM

Wire received. Coming down with unsigned warrant. Arrive five-forty. LESTRADE.

REPLIES BY TELEGRAPH, or other telegrams, may be handed to messenger

INSPECTOR LESTRADE
A POLICE DETECTIVE WHO CONSULTS SHERLOCK HOLMES ON MANY CASES

"He is the best of the professionals, I think, and we may need his assistance. Now, Watson, I think that we cannot employ our time better than by calling upon your acquaintance, Mrs Laura Lyons."

COOMBE TRACEY

Mrs Laura Lyons was in her office, and Sherlock Holmes opened his interview with a frankness and directness which considerably amazed her.

"I am investigating the circumstances which attended the death of the late SIR CHARLES BASKERVILLE," said he. "We regard this case as one of MURDER, and the evidence may implicate not only your friend Mr Stapleton, but his *wife* as well."

The lady sprang from her chair.

His **WIFE!**

she cried.

"The person who has passed for his sister is really his wife," said Holmes.

Mrs Lyons had resumed her seat. Her hands were grasping the arms of her chair, and I saw that the pink nails had turned white with the pressure of her grip.

His wife! she said again.

His *wife*!
Prove it to me!
And if you can
do so –!

The fierce flash of her eyes said more than any words.

"I have come prepared to do so," said Holmes, drawing several papers from his pocket.

"Here is a photograph of the couple taken in York four years ago. It is indorsed 'Mr and Mrs Vandeleur,' but you will have no difficulty in recognising him, and her also, if you know her by sight."

"Mr Holmes," she said, "this man had offered me marriage on condition that I could get a divorce from my

Mr and Mrs Vandeleur

husband. He has lied to me, the villain, in every conceivable way. Ask me what you like, and there is nothing which I shall hold back."

One thing I swear to you, and that is that when I wrote the letter I never dreamed of any harm to Sir Charles, who had been my kindest friend.

"I entirely believe you, madam," said Sherlock Holmes. "The sending of this letter was suggested to you by Stapleton?"

"He dictated it."

IT'S A MYSTERY!
THE LETTER
It was sent by Laura Lyons – all because Stapleton told her to

MYSTERY SOLVED!

I presume that the reason he gave was that you would receive help from Sir Charles for the legal expenses connected with your divorce?

Exactly.

"And then after you had sent the letter he dissuaded you from keeping the appointment?"

"He told me that it would hurt his self-respect."

"And then you heard nothing until you read the reports of the death in the paper?"

"No."

"And he made you swear to say nothing about your appointment with Sir Charles?"

"He did. He said that the death was a very mysterious one, and that I should certainly be suspected if the facts came out. He frightened me into remaining silent."

"You have had a fortunate escape," said Sherlock Holmes. "You have had him in your power and he knew it, and yet you are alive. You have been walking for some months very near to the edge of a precipice."

"Are you armed, Lestrade?"

The little detective smiled.

As long as I have my trousers I have a hip-pocket, and as long as I have my hip-pocket I have something in it.

Good! My friend and I are also ready for emergencies.

The wagonette was paid off and ordered to return to Coombe Tracey forthwith, while we started to walk to Merripit House.

"You're mighty close about this affair, Mr Holmes. What's the game now?"

"A waiting game."

"My word, it does not seem a very cheerful place," said the detective with a shiver, glancing round him at the gloomy slopes of the hill and at the huge lake of fog which lay over the Grimpen Mire. "I see the lights of a house ahead of us."

"That is Merripit House and the end of our journey. I must request you to walk on tiptoe and not to talk above a whisper."

We moved cautiously along the track as if we were bound for the house, but Holmes halted us when we were about two hundred yards from it.

This will do, said he.

These rocks upon the right make an admirable screen.

He dropped on his knees and clapped his ear to the ground.

Thank God, I think that I hear him coming.

A sound of quick steps broke the silence of the moor. The steps grew louder, and through the fog, as through a curtain, there stepped the man whom we were awaiting.

Sir Henry looked round him as he emerged into the clear, starlit night. Then he came swiftly along the path, passed close to where we lay, and went on up the long slope behind us. As he walked he glanced continually over either shoulder, like a man who is ill at ease.

Hist! cried Holmes, and I heard the sharp **CLICK** of his pistol.

LOOK OUT! It's coming!

There was a thin, crisp, continuous patter from somewhere in the heart of that crawling bank.

The cloud was within fifty yards of where we lay, and we glared at it, uncertain what horror was about to break from the heart of it.

I was at Holmes's elbow, and I glanced for an instant at his face. It was pale and exultant, his eyes shining brightly in the moonlight.

"The blinds are up. You know the lie of the land best. Creep forward quietly and see what they are doing – but for heaven's sake don't let them know that they are watched!"

I tiptoed down the path and reached a point whence I could look straight through the uncurtained window.

There were only two men in the room, Sir Henry and Stapleton. They sat with their profiles towards me on either side of the round table. Both of them were smoking cigars, and coffee and wine were in front of them.

Stapleton was talking with animation, but Sir Henry looked pale. Perhaps the thought of that

"We are to wait here?"

"Yes, we shall make our little ambush here. Get into this hollow, Lestrade. You have been inside the house, have you not, Watson? Can you tell the position of the rooms? What are those latticed windows at this end?"

"I think they are the kitchen windows."

"And the one beyond, which shines so brightly?"

"That is certainly the dining-room."

lonely walk across the ill-omened moor was weighing heavily upon his mind.

As I watched them Stapleton rose and left the room. I heard the creak of a door and the crisp sound of boots upon gravel. Looking over, I saw the naturalist pause at the door of an out-house in the corner of the orchard. A key turned in a lock, and as he passed in there was a curious scuffling noise from within.

He was only a minute or so inside, and then I heard the key turn once more and he passed me and re-entered the house.

I saw him rejoin his guest, and I crept quietly back to where my companions were waiting to tell them what I had seen.

Over the great Grimpen Mire there hung a dense, white fog.

It was drifting slowly in our direction, low, but thick and well defined. The moon shone on it, and it looked like a great shimmering ice-field.

"It's moving towards us, Watson – the one thing upon earth which could have disarranged my plans. He can't be very long, now. It is already ten o'clock. Our success and even his life may depend upon his coming out before the fog is over the path," Holmes muttered impatiently.

The night was clear and fine above us.
Before us lay the dark bulk of the house,
hard outlined against the silver-spangled sky.
Broad bars of golden light from the lower
windows stretched across the orchard and
the moor. One of them was suddenly shut
off. The servants had left the kitchen.
There only remained the lamp in the
dining-room where the two men,
the murderous host and the guest,
still chatted over
their cigars.

Every minute that white woolly plain which covered one half of the moor was drifting closer and closer to the house. Already the first thin wisps of it were curling across the golden square of the lighted window.

The fog-wreaths came crawling round both corners of the house and rolled slowly into one dense bank, on which the upper floor and the roof floated like a strange ship upon a shadowy sea. Holmes struck his hand passionately upon the rock in front of us and stamped his feet in his impatience.

If he isn't out in a quarter of an hour the path will be covered. In half an hour we won't be able to see our hands in front of us.

NOW TO MEET INSPECTOR LESTRADE

The London express came roaring into the station, and a small, wiry bulldog of a man sprang from a first-class carriage. We all three shook hands.

Anything good? asked Lestrade.

The biggest thing for years, said Holmes.

"We have two hours before we need think of starting. I think we might employ it in getting some dinner and then, Lestrade, we will take the London fog out of your throat by giving you a breath of the pure night air of Dartmoor. Never been there? Ah, well, I don't suppose you will forget your first visit."

CHAPTER

18

The HOUND of the
BASKERVILLES

THE GREAT ORDEAL was in front of us. My nerves thrilled with anticipation when at last the cold wind upon our faces and the dark spaces on either side of the narrow road told me that we were back upon the moor once again.

Every stride of the horses and every turn of the wheels was taking us nearer to our supreme adventure.

But suddenly they started forward in a rigid, fixed stare, and his lips parted in amazement.

At the same instant Lestrade gave a yell of terror

!!!

and threw himself face downward upon the ground.

Yikes!

I sprang to my feet, my inert hand grasping my pistol, my mind paralysed by the dreadful shape which had sprung out upon us from the shadows of the fog.

IT WAS, AN **ENORMOUS COAL-BLACK HOUND,**

but not such a hound as mortal eyes have ever seen.

FIRE burst from its open mouth,

its eyes glowed with a smouldering glare,

its muzzle and hackles and dewlap were outlined in flickering flame.

Never in the delirious dream of a disordered brain could anything more savage,

more appalling,

more hellish

be conceived

than that dark form and savage face
which broke upon us out of the wall of fog.

With long bounds the huge black creature was leaping down the track, following hard upon the footsteps of our friend.

Holmes and I both fired together, and the creature gave a hideous howl.

He did not pause, however, but bounded onward.

Far away on the path we saw Sir Henry looking back, his hands raised in horror, glaring helplessly at the frightful thing which was hunting him down.

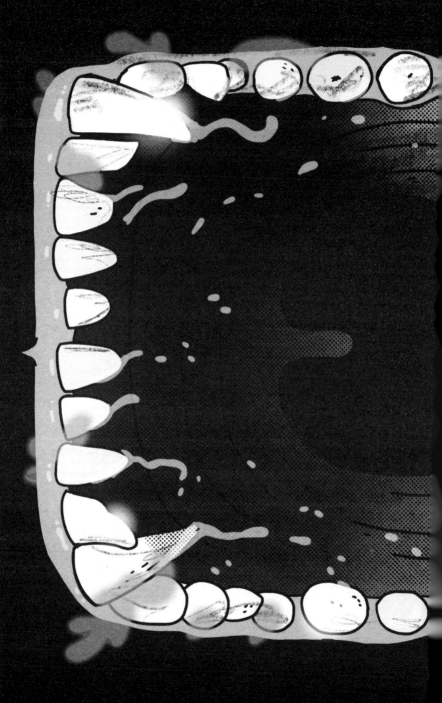

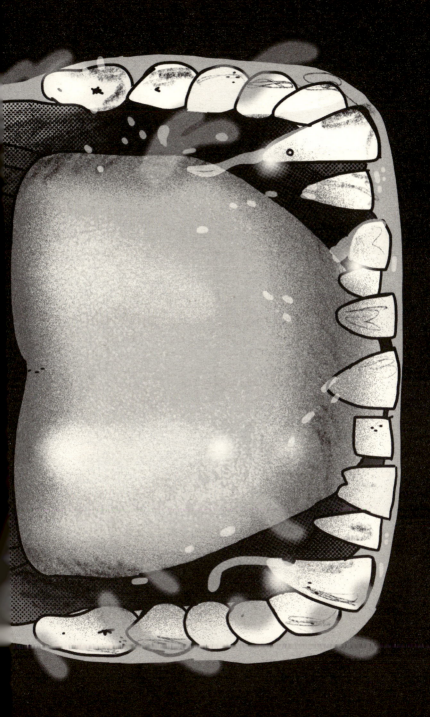

Never have I seen a man run as Holmes ran that night.

In front of us as we flew up the track we heard

SCREAM

SCREAM SCREAM SCREAM SCREAM SCREAM SCREAM SCREAM SCREAM

SCREAM SCREAM SCREAM SCREAM SCREAM SCREAM SCREAM SCREAM

AFTER

SCREAM

FROM SIR HENRY

and the deep roar of the hound.

I was in time to see the beast spring upon its victim.

CHOMP!

But the next instant Holmes had emptied five barrels of his revolver into the creature's flank.

BANG!
BANG!
BANG!
BANG!
BANG!

With a last howl of agony and a vicious snap in the air, it rolled upon its back, four feet pawing furiously, and then fell limp upon its side.

THE GIANT HOUND WAS DEAD.

CHAPTER
19
THE VILLAIN

SIR HENRY LAY insensible where he had fallen. We tore away his collar, and Holmes breathed a prayer of gratitude when we saw that there was no sign of a wound and that the rescue had been in time. Already our friend's eyelids shivered and he made a feeble effort to move.

What *was* it?

he whispered.

What, in heaven's name, was it?

"It's dead, whatever it is," said Holmes. "We've laid the family ghost once and forever."

In mere size and strength it was a terrible creature which was lying stretched before us. It was gaunt, savage, and as large as a small lioness. The huge jaws seemed to be dripping with a flame and the small, deep-set, cruel eyes were ringed with fire.

I placed my hand upon the glowing muzzle, and as I held them up my own fingers smouldered and gleamed in the darkness.

Phosphorus, I said.

"A cunning preparation of it," said Holmes, sniffing at the dead animal. "There is no smell which might have interfered with his power of scent. We owe you a deep apology, Sir Henry, for having exposed you to this fright. I was prepared for a HOUND, but not for such a creature as this."

PHOSPHORUS

A chemical element that glows when it is exposed to oxygen. So the hound is not a devilish beast, but just a very big dog and Stapleton had used phosphorus to make it look extra scary.

You have saved
my life.

He tried to stagger to his feet.
We helped him to a rock, where
he sat shivering with his face
buried in his hands.

"We must leave you now," said Holmes.
"The rest of our work must be done, and every
moment is of importance. We have our case, and
now we only want our man."

The front door was open, so we rushed in. Holmes caught up the lamp and left no corner of the house unexplored.

No sign could we see of the man whom we were chasing.

On the upper floor, however, one of the bedroom doors was locked.

A faint moaning and rustling came from within.

Holmes struck the door and it flew open.
Pistol in hand, we all three rushed into the room.

The room had been
fashioned into a
small museum, and
the walls were lined
by a number of
glass-topped cases
full of butterflies
and moths.

In the centre of
this room there
was an upright
beam. To this
post a figure
was tied, swathed
and muffled.

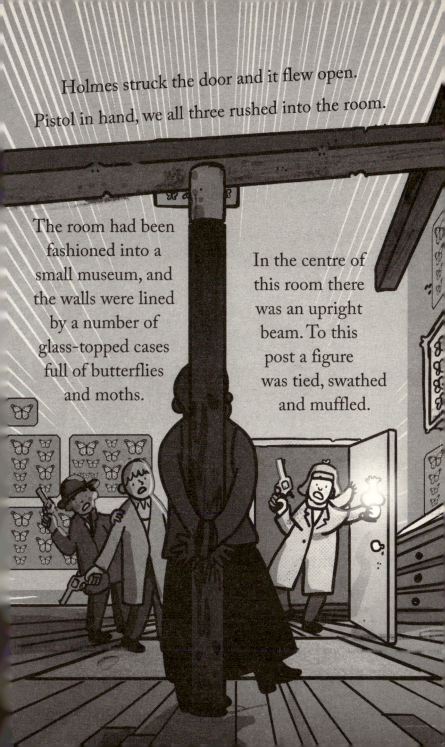

In a minute we had torn off the gag, unswathed the bonds, and Mrs Stapleton sank upon the floor in front of us.

Is he safe? she asked.

Has he escaped?

He cannot escape us, madam.

"No, no, I did not mean my husband. Sir Henry? Is he safe?"

"Yes."

"And the hound?"

"It is dead."

She gave a long sigh of satisfaction.

"Thank God! Thank God! Oh, this villain!

See how he has treated me!" She broke into passionate sobbing as she spoke.

"You bear him no good will, madam," said Holmes. "Tell us then where we shall find him."

"There is but one place where he can have fled," she answered.

"There is an old tin mine on an island in the heart of the mire. It was there that he kept his hound and there also he had made

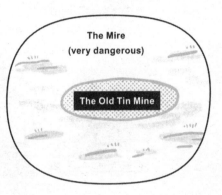

preparations so that he might have a refuge. That is where he would fly."

It was evident to us that all pursuit was in vain until the fog had lifted. Meanwhile we left Lestrade at the house while Holmes and I went back with Sir Henry to Baskerville Hall.

CHAPTER
❧ 20 ❧
THE FINAL CHAPTER

AND NOW I come rapidly to the conclusion of this singular narrative.

Squelch-squerch!

On the morning after the death of the hound the fog had lifted and we were guided by Mrs Stapleton to the point where the path zigzagged from tuft to tuft of rushes among those green-scummed pits and foul quagmires which barred the way to the stranger.

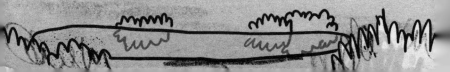

Rank reeds and lush, slimy water-plants sent an odour of decay, while a false step plunged us more than once thigh-deep into the dark, quivering mire, as if some malignant hand was tugging us down into those obscene depths.

From amid a tuft of cotton grass some dark thing was projecting out of the slime.

Holmes sank to his waist as he stepped from the path to seize it, and had we not been there to drag him out he could never have set his foot upon firm land again.

He held an old black boot in the air.

It is worth a mud bath,

said he.

It is our friend Sir Henry's missing boot.

"Thrown there by Stapleton in his flight."

"Exactly. He retained it in his hand after using it to set the hound upon Sir Henry's track."

Here boy, smell this. This is the smell of your victim!

Sniff!

But more than that we were never destined to know. There was no chance of finding footsteps in the mire. If the earth told a true story, then Stapleton never reached that island of refuge.

Somewhere in the heart of the great Grimpen Mire, down in the foul slime of the huge morass which had sucked him in,

this cold
and
cruel-hearted
man
is
forever
buried.

ENDS

ARTHUR CONAN DOYLE

(1859 – 1930)

Arthur Conan Doyle was a prolific Scottish author and doctor best known for creating the beloved characters of Sherlock Holmes and Dr Watson. While the detective duo are his most famous work, he's written lots of other books, including fantasy, science fiction and non-fiction.

Sherlock Holmes first appeared in 1887 in *A Study in Scarlet* and his name has been known all over the world since!

JACK NOEL

(1984 – ???)

Jack Noel is a writer
and illustrator. In 1986 he won a
beautiful baby competition. In 1996
he ate ten Weetabix in one sitting.

As well as doodling throughout
great works of literature, Jack has
written a book all by himself, called
My Headteacher is an Evil Genius.
It's all about a headteacher that's
an evil genius. You'd like it!

He lives in London with his
wife and two kids.

@jackdraws

ARTHUR CONAN DOYLE

He based Sherlock Holmes on his teacher

Doyle was inspired by his university lecturer, Dr Joseph Bell, who was a master at deducing facts from tiny detail. Sherlock even looked a little like Dr Bell. *The Adventures of Sherlock Holmes* is dedicated to Dr Bell who said of Doyle: "You are yourself Sherlock Holmes and well you know it."

He solved some real-life crimes cases himself

Like Sherlock Holmes, Doyle dabbled in cracking cases on the side. Most famously, he helped overturn a conviction against Oscar Slater, who had been serving two decades in prison for a murder he didn't commit. Doyle tirelessly campaigned for his release and even wrote *The Case of Oscar Slater* as a plea for Slater's pardon.

He played cricket and football

Doyle was great at sports and played on the same cricket team as JM Barrie, the celebrated author of *Peter Pan*.

He knew famous magician Harry Houdini

Houdini and Doyle were friends, due to their mutual interest in spiritualism (where the dead can speak to the living). Their unlikely friendship lasted until 1922, when Doyle and his wife held a séance to contact Houdini's dead mother. But when they showed him a letter allegedly from his mother as proof, Houdini was outraged – the letter was written in English, a language his mother didn't speak!

He believed in fairies!

In the 1920s, when two young girls, Elsie Wright and Frances Griffiths, shared photos of themselves surrounded by fairies, Doyle was one of the people who believed that it was proof that fairies and spirits were real. He used these to illustrate an article he'd written, *The Evidence for Fairies*, and later a book called *The Coming of the Fairies*.